WHEN THE CIRCUS CAME TO TOWN

FARRAR
STRAUS
GIROUX

Also by
POLLY HORVATH

An Occasional Cow
with pictures by Gioia Fiammenghi

No More Cornflakes

The Happy Yellow Car

POLLY HORVATH

When the Circus Came to Town

Farrar Straus Giroux
New York

For Sally

Copyright © 1996 by Polly Horvath
All rights reserved
Published simultaneously in Canada by
HarperCollins*CanadaLtd*
Printed in the United States of America
Designed by Lilian Rosenstreich
First edition, 1996

Library of Congress Cataloging-in-Publication Data
Horvath, Polly.
When the circus came to town / Polly Horvath. — 1st ed.
p.   cm.
[1. Circus—Fiction.   2. Prejudices—Fiction.
3. Friendship—Fiction.   4. Family life—Fiction.]
I. Title
PZ7.H97224Wh 1996 [Fic]—dc20 96-11591 CIP AC

WHEN THE CIRCUS CAME TO TOWN

One

I WILL NEVER FORGET the day of the night that I first saw the Halibuts. It was a bright snowy March day and I lay in bed staring at dust particles swirling, swirling, swirling in a ray of sunshine. Then I looked out the window at the vacant house next door. A large SOLD sign was posted in front. I waited as I always did to see if anyone would come in or out of it. When no one did, I went back to the dust particles. It wasn't much, but it passed the time.

I had pneumonia and had been in the house now for thirty-two days two hours and seventeen minutes. I didn't count seconds. For some time before being bedridden, I had been coughing around school, but since I wasn't dripping blood from every pore, a month had passed before my mom carted me off to a doctor, who after a chest X ray confirmed that I was sick. I had been getting around okay up to that point, but as soon as I got the diagnosis, I relaxed and ran a fever of 105. Those days and nights are kind of foggy, but I do remember thinking that it would be a shame if I died before I finished writing my novel.

I wasn't feeling strong and I could not lift a heavy pencil to attack my homework. My manuscript, however, had to be done. I was just devising a series of weights and pulleys for my pencil when I spotted a Grendel's truck parking in front of the house next door. Grendel's is the department store downtown. Aha, I thought, the new people are finally moving in and they must have purchased something. A washer perhaps? A dryer? I sat up slowly on my pillows and tried to see what it was they were uncrating. But it wasn't one thing—it was roomful after roomful of furniture. This new family had apparently completely furnished their house from Grendel's. Had they never owned anything? Perhaps they were from far away and it was cheaper to start over with new stuff. Or perhaps they were a newlywed rich couple. My mother came into my room at that moment with a bowl of chicken-noodle soup.

"Outta my way," I said without thinking, as she stood in front of the window to serve it to me.

"Ivy!" said my mother reproachfully.

"Look, look," I explained. "Someone is moving into the house next door."

My mother put the soup down and it slopped on the blankets. I love my mother but she isn't a Betty Crocker mother. It isn't that she doesn't cook or clean. She's a good cook and our house is tidy as can be, but she doesn't have a Betty Crocker attitude and when she opens her mouth neat little sayings don't come flying out.

"Have you seen the new neighbors yet?" she asked, absentmindedly mopping the blanket with my used-to-be-clean bathrobe.

"No and they've moved about eighteen rooms of furniture into the house already."

"The Wilsons' house only has nine rooms," said my mother. The Wilsons were the family who used to live there.

"Perhaps they are keeping some for spare," I said. "Perhaps they will whip out a new bed should someone, say, spill chicken-noodle soup on it."

"Hmmm," said my mother, who wasn't paying any attention to me. "Look at that living-room set. They seem to like mostly reds and yellows. Can you imagine a living room in red and yellow?"

"Oh for yuk," I said. A young rich couple with terrible taste. It was just what the neighborhood needed. I hoped they had some eccentric habits, too, like hunting squirrels in their underwear.

"Circus colors," said my mother thoughtfully. "Well, I wonder when they plan to move in. Surely today. In fact, someone must be there now directing traffic. Maybe I'll just whip over with some brownies."

"Yes, do," I said. "But first you might toss me a couple."

"I'm glad to see you getting your appetite back," said my mother, pulling the chicken-soup blankets off my bed to take down to the laundry with my bathrobe.

I watched spellbound through the window as my mother trotted over, looking very ordinary and efficient, a plate of brownies in hand. I saw her talking to the men moving in the furniture. Then she trotted back, brownies intact. She came right up to my bedroom without even taking off her coat.

"Well, they're not there. They gave Grendel's a key and a *floor plan* of how they wanted their furniture placed. They don't get in until tonight. I asked the moving men what the family's name was and they wouldn't tell me, so I wouldn't give them a single brownie. Here, have one," said my mother, reaching under the foil cover and eating one herself. My only clean blanket was now filled with chocolate crumbs, but I didn't mind. It would give me many happy hours of search and rescue.

When the last stick of furniture had been delivered and the Grendel's truck had pulled out, my mother and I sighed.

"Well, they should be all set for their first night," said my mother.

"Of course, they had still better be prepared to make beds and unpack dishes and stuff," I said. "There must be another truck coming with their other things."

"Or they're bringing it with them in a U-Haul or something," said my mother.

We licked the crumbs off our fingers and kept staring outside until the phone rang and my mother got up, taking the brownies with her.

At suppertime my father arrived home and, as usual, came upstairs to see me first. He smelled of cigars and fresh air. "How is my poor bedraggled daughter?" he boomed. I smiled wanly and he gave me a large bone-crushing hug before going down to see my mother. My father is a banker. He loves it. I don't think there is anything about my father's life that he doesn't give his whole heart to. He adores my mother, whom he calls Marie Antoinette. He adores me, his bedraggled daughter, B.D. for short. I don't know why he calls me that, I'm really very neat. He loves his work, our town of Springfield, the whole darn United States of America. Sometimes I feel I must protect him in his happiness. If a burglar came into the house, for instance, he might embrace him, too. So I keep a sharp lookout.

After a dinner of yet more chicken-noodle soup, my mother brought up my clean blankets and bathrobe and that was it for the night. I turned off the lights and lay in the dark listening for the new neighbors' arrival. I was afraid I would be asleep if they didn't hurry up, but finally I heard a car park in front of the house. I hitched myself up and wished I had my binoculars handy. It was too dark to see the figures clearly, but it looked as if the family consisted of a tall, broad-shouldered man, a short, squat woman, and a child. They carried in suitcases, shut the door, and turned on the lights. For a while I watched the different lights go on and off in different rooms. I kept hoping they would go back out to the car for something, but they didn't.

Two

THE NEXT DAY the new neighbors appeared in day-
light to unload their car and I had to make a few ad-
justments. By now I had my binoculars and could see
that the man was the short and solid one. He had a
long handlebar mustache which curved around his
nose. The woman was tall and broad-shouldered, with
a better-to-eat-you-with smile. I had never seen so
many choppers in one mouth. There must have been
nine or ten extra in there easy. Then the child came
out. It was a boy. I would have preferred a girl but boys
are okay if they behave themselves and don't start any
of those games that end with everyone going to the
hospital.

My mother came into my room bearing a bowl of
tapioca. She believes tapioca can cure anything.

"Here to baptize my blankets again?" I asked offhandedly as she plopped down on my bed, handed me the tapioca, and grabbed the binoculars.

"You don't need those," I said. *"You* can go over, brownies in hand, and ask questions. Now, I happen to have made a small list for you."

She read it out loud. "Are any of your ancestors Vikings? Who are you? Do you have any plans to buy one of those dogs that bark loudly all night long? Why are you here? Do you sometimes find yourself treating all the neighborhood children to ice cream just because you can't resist the ding-a-ling sound of the truck?" She smiled politely and pocketed the list.

"As you can see," I said, "I cleverly inserted the really important questions among some good conversation starters."

My mother picked up the binoculars again and gazed through them. "They certainly are an odd-looking couple."

"Why don't you go over with the brownies?" I suggested.

"There are only two left," said my mother, still peering through the binoculars.

"Two!"

"Your father was hungry."

"Well, don't you have anything else you could take over? A selection of fruit and cheese perhaps?"

"There's a piece of moldy Velveeta in the back of the fridge," my mother said. "Do you think they'd want that?"

"Ugh," I said, spooning up tapioca. "If you know it's moldy, why don't you throw it out?"

"These things have to be done del-i-cate-ly," said my mother, cackling. "Maybe I'll go over and offer to help them carry things in."

"Well, you had better hurry. It doesn't look like they have much left."

My mother leapt up, raced down the stairs, out the front door, and started to jog over. She must have realized how it looked because she slowed to a brisk-friendly-harmless walk. I couldn't hear what they were saying but there was a lot of smiling, handshaking, and pointing to our house. Then the boy looked up and saw me. I immediately fell back and put a pillow over my head. I hoped that if I didn't move he would come to the conclusion that I had been a figment of his imagination. After a while my mom came home and right upstairs.

"Well," she said, breathlessly dropping on my bed and talking to my pillow, "Their name is Halibut. Remember I said that their living-room set had circus colors? Do you remember that?"

All I could think was that Halibut was a very odd name.

"Well?" said my mother, impatiently bouncing up and down. Had she forgotten that I was at death's door? "Do you remember?"

"I remember. Please stop bouncing. It's making me queasy," I said, taking the pillow off my face.

"Guess what he does for a living?" she asked.

"He works for the circus," I said. You might say she had kind of given it away.

Worked for the circus, did he? A sudden thought occurred to me. But no, it was too bizarre. Too Twilight-Zone.

"Well, well, well," I said to my mother, yawning. "I think I need a nap. Yep, that's it, a nap. Sleep. Some quiet time. Ho." I paused dramatically. "Hum." I sank into the pillows and she tiptoed out.

As soon as she was gone, I reached under the bed and took out my manuscript. A delightful novel, all about a family who moves to a small town. The father is small and round, the mother is big, but the child in my book was a girl. No matter. Their name was Clancey, not Halibut, true, *but the father worked for the circus!* It was swiftly becoming apparent to me that the family I had created had moved in next door.

I picked up the binoculars and looked across the way. The mother was in the kitchen, loading pots and pans into the cupboards. The father was putting things into a whatnot. Where was the boy? As I studied the upstairs windows I had a creepy feeling, a person-looking-over-your-shoulder type of feeling, and moving over one window I found myself staring into someone else's binoculars. The nerve. I dropped my binoculars and slammed down my shade.

Later in the morning my mother called up, "Letter for you, Ivy!"

This was a surprise. No one ever wrote me letters,

probably because I didn't have any friends. The occasional acquaintance invited me to a birthday party or Halloween celebration but I had never had the kind of friendship where you bare your soul, and no one had ever bared their soul to me. At least as far as I knew.

"I wonder who it could be from," I said to my mother when she sprang in and tossed it to me.

"It's from the little boy next door," she said.

So much for surprises. I ripped open the envelope.

"Dear Ivy," it began.

"How does he know my name?" I asked my mother.

"Oh, I told them all about you when I was over. What school you went to and that you'd been in bed with pneumonia for a month and that you're a writer."

"As if they didn't know," I said, snorting. After all, these were my book characters we were talking about.

"Why in the world would they know any of that, Ivy?" asked my mother. "Aren't you going to read your letter?"

Ah yes, the letter.

Dear Ivy

Your mother told us that you are sick. I told your mother who my teacher was going to be and she said we will be in the same fifth-grade class. I start school on Monday. I have never been in a school before.

(Well, how many book characters have, I thought.)

We have always traveled with the circus and I have
been home-schooled. If you get out your binoculars and
wave hi, I will too.

(Ah, a friendly sort.)

Your neighbor
Alfred Halibut
P.S. Did I tell you about my mother and the tooth
fairy?

Did he tell me about his mother and the tooth fairy?
Couldn't he just reread his letter and find out?

I looked at my mother.

"Well?" she asked. "I suspect he's lonely. Maybe we
should invite him over."

I gazed at her in horror.

"Dr. Nipon said that you could get up and move
about a bit when you felt better," said my mother de-
fensively. "And you do look better. Your color is better. You're eating better. Maybe you would feel more
lively if you got dressed for a short period every day and
we propped you on some pillows downstairs."

In truth, the idea had appeal. I was tired of looking
at the dust particles, but I wasn't quite ready to give
up my claim to massive amounts of sympthy and
T.L.C. I had a feeling that once I moved downstairs
I was going to be expected to get my own tapioca.

"My strength is fading," I said, sitting back on the
pillows and closing my eyes.

"Well, think about it," said my mother. "I'll even play Monopoly with you."

I opened one weary eye. "We could play that on my bed."

"The pieces would slip off and we'd lose hotels in the covers. You need a flat surface."

"Perhaps later," I said in a weak voice meant to create doubt as to whether my strength would hold out that long. I sank back into feigned sleep and my mother, ever cat-like, disappeared on little fog feet.

I took my binoculars and very, very slowly directed them upwards over the window ledge, hoping to see without being seen. When I finally located Alfred's room, his bony fingers were right there, fluttering in a wave.

Three

BY MID-AFTERNOON I was lying on the couch downstairs in a sweatsuit with an afghan draped artistic-
ally about my knees and a cup of Ovaltine in my hand.

"Howya doin'?" called my mother from the kitchen.

"More marshmallows, please."

My mother breezed through, plopping a handful in
my cup. She was heading next door with an invitation
for Alfred to come over and expose himself to double
pneumonia.

"I'll be back in a minute. Now, you're sure you're up
to this?" My mother had tried calling, but the Halibuts
didn't have a phone yet. She tied a scarf around her
neck. The temperature had suddenly gone down to
twenty below and even a trip next door was fraught
with lurking frostbite dangers.

"I'll try to be strong," I said, letting my voice trail off.

My mother threw me a look and I settled into my pillows. Under them I had hidden my notebook and pencil. I wanted to get on with my book about the Clanceys, but first I needed to broach the subject with Alfred. Did he know he was fictional?

They were back before I had figured out how to deal with Alfred. He came in looking sheepish and shy. He had a long shock of black hair that fell over his eyes and he was short for his age. He would, in fact, be the shortest person in our class. He took off his snowy boots and my mother hung up his jacket while talking a mile a minute to cover up his shyness.

"Oh, Iiiiivy . . ." she called sweetly as if I were in the next state instead of ten feet away on the couch. "Iiiivy, dear, here's Alfred. Alfred, this is Ivy."

I thought he was peering at me from behind his hair but it was hard to tell.

"Hi," I said.

He mumbled something indistinct.

"Wouldn't you like some Ovaltine?" asked my mother, bustling toward the kitchen. "Just go and sit anywhere. Ivy likes Ovaltine. She would drink it all day and night if I let her, which of course I don't, because you know what they say about too much of a good thing, and anything with caffeine will eventually turn you into a nervous sort of person, don't you think? We have some marshmallows, those mini-kind, the colored ones? They're kind of disgusting really if you think about it which maybe we better not stop and do."

Alfred started to make odd throat-clearing noises, "honk, honk, gurgle." Was he warming up for speech, I thought in my usual grumpy way, or was he, in fact, a car? "Yes, please," he finally spat out.

When my mother had left the room I told Alfred to sit down and pointed to the rocking chair. I wasn't trying to be bossy but he did seem in need of some kind of direction. He went over and sat on the edge of it. I could see what his problem was: he was looking down at the snow on the cuffs of his pants. It was slowly melting and dripping on the floor.

"Don't worry about the puddle," I said. "This kind of thick shag carpeting just absorbs it. Everyone is always bringing in snow. It's kind of a cheap form of carpet cleaning."

"So, school on Monday!" he said.

"Well, you'll probably like our teacher. She's pretty good," I said reassuringly while I tried to figure out a tactful way to bring up what might be a painful subject for him—i.e., that I had *written* him.

"I guess," he said. "I have no basis for comparison."

My mother came in with his Ovaltine and sat down. Oh fudge, I thought. I could hardly bring up the subject of his fictional nature with her hanging on every word.

I looked at my empty cup. "Could I have some more, too?" I asked. When she had gone into the kitchen, I hobbled in after her and hissed, "Maybe you could go upstairs. He's really shy and I can't talk to him with you there."

"Oh," whispered my mother, nodding emphatically. "Of course. I'll just go up and practice my lute."

My mother was taking lute lessons. She had joined a group of lute players at the church who played for the services. They called themselves Lutes for Lent.

I brought my own Ovaltine into the living room and my mother deposited a plate of her peanut-butter chocolate-chip cookies on the table and left the room, giving Alfred what I'm sure were meant to be many big, welcoming, reassuring smiles, but she looked more like someone trying to pretend she doesn't see that your nose is about to fall off.

Alfred sipped his Ovaltine self-consciously, his shock of hair just fractions of an inch from dipping into it. It fascinated me so much that I couldn't think what to say. When the lute music started, Alfred glanced up in surprise, but without chocolaty bangs. I guessed he had gotten pretty good at judging how close he could come without getting them wet.

"Have a cookie?" I asked, holding up the plate. He reached forward and took one, nearly upsetting his Ovaltine and the rocking chair, and then sat back, trying to fold up like a concertina.

"So," I said. "Your dad works for the circus?"

"Publicity manager," he said. "He used to work for a small circus that didn't have much money for advertising, so he didn't make much money, and we all traveled with the circus. But now he works for a big circus. He still has to travel with them a lot but we can finally afford a house."

"That's nice," I said. "How much of your life do you remember before, say, Saturday?" I had decided that this was the most tactful way to see if he knew that his life had been up until yesterday four short chapters in the book I was writing.

He stopped eating and looked at me, flicking his hair out of his eyes with a jerk of his head. "How much of my *life* do I remember? I guess back until I was four. How much of *your* life do you remember?"

"More than four short chapters," I said, taking a cookie and chewing meaningly.

"Chapters?" he began but stopped as the lute music got louder and louder. "What is that sound?"

"My mother plays the lute," I said. "Does your mother play an instrument?"

"No," said Alfred. "But she knits rhythmically."

I couldn't tell if he was joking or not. His hair was back over his face. When you could see his features, they were sharp and foxlike.

"So, what's this you were dying to tell me about your mother and the tooth fairy?" I said, getting out my pencil and paper.

"What are you doing?" he asked, looking for some place to deposit his empty cup.

"Put it on the windowsill," I directed. "I am taking notes. I'm a writer." I let this sink in.

"That's an odd coincidence," he said.

Aha! "Yes, I'm a writer, you're a character," I said, thinking, *The ball is in your court, bud.*

"What do you mean?" he asked.

Maybe he really didn't know he was fictional. "Well," I said gently, "I'm going to write a book and put you in it."

"You don't even know me," he said.

"Doesn't matter. You'll do," I said, feeling flustered.

"Can't you just make up someone?" he asked.

"I think I'll write about your mother and the tooth fairy," I said. "I will chuck my old chapter 4 and you can be my new chapter 4."

"I don't want to be chapter 4," he said.

"Whatever you say," I said, agreeable to the end.

Four

"*WELL,*" *ALFRED BEGAN,* "I lost my last bicuspid yesterday on the train coming here."

"I thought you arrived by car," I said, scribbling madly.

"No, my mom and I took the train, because my dad had to make a number of stops and take care of publicity stuff in some towns along the way. He picked us up at the station. Anyhow, I lost my last bicuspid."

"Aren't you a little *old* to be shedding bicuspids all over Amtrak?" I asked. I had planned to write things down as he said them, without asking questions or making comments, but I kind of liked talking to him and I could see this was going to take us on little diversions.

"All of my family loses their teeth late," he said, raising his eyebrows challengingly.

"Except your mom, who doesn't look as if she ever lost any," I said.

"I'm getting to that," he said. "You're not going to get a very coherent story if you keep interrupting every three minutes." He flipped his hair out of his eyes. He was probably right to keep them covered most of the time. They were disconcertingly piercing.

"Sorry, sorry," I said.

"Well, I had the bloody bicuspid in a Kleenex on my lap and I asked my mother—jokingly, of course—if the tooth fairy was going to come that night. Naturally, I don't believe in the tooth fairy anymore, but you know how they want you to keep believing in things and you don't like to disappoint them?"

I nodded. I was amazed. I thought I was the only one who pretended to believe in things so as not to hurt my parents' feelings. I chewed my pencil eraser. "So, did you put your tooth under your pillow?"

"That's when things got all mixed up, because my mom said I *shouldn't* put it under my pillow. That when she was my age she put a tooth under her pillow, and instead of getting a shiny new dime, the tooth fairy came and rammed sixteen extra teeth into my mother's mouth, which she has had to accommodate ever since."

I was writing furiously but I stopped and looked up. "Wait a second, you don't believe in a good tooth fairy who delivers dimes but you do believe in an evil tooth fairy that delivers extra teeth?"

"Well," said Alfred, "if you don't believe in a good tooth fairy, what harm does it do? But who wants to take a risk with a bad tooth fairy? Can you imagine what I would look like with another sixteen teeth?"

"Alfred, is it possible that your mother is tired of handing out dimes for teeth?"

"Certainly not," said Alfred coldly.

"There's only one way to be sure," I said, putting down my pencil. "Tonight you are going to put that tooth under your pillow."

"I am not," said Alfred. "And even if I wanted to, I've already thrown it out, so there's no chance the tooth fairy will ever find me."

"Never mind, I can get you a tooth," I said. I ran upstairs to my room as swiftly as I could on wobbly legs and got out my tooth jar from my desk drawer. I always asked for the tooth fairy to return my teeth because I was collecting them. She, or rather my mom, always did return them the night after to the little baby-food jar I had specified. My mother said, honestly, what did I need them for, but clearly she never foresaw this day. I selected a bicuspid and ran back down.

"Here," I said, holding it out to him. "A tooth to put under your pillow."

He didn't exactly leap at this generous offer but sat rather nonchalantly on his hands.

"Oh, come on, it doesn't have cooties," I said, sighing, and got Alfred an envelope. Just then the doorbell rang. It was his mother. She had come to collect him. I smiled at her but she frightened me. She must have been almost six feet tall and she had feet like barges at the end of her legs. I wondered if she could possibly find shoes at a normal shoe store.

"Ivy!" she said. "I've heard so much about you."

Alfred sucked his head into his shoulders, making his neck a thing of the past. He had been quite forthcoming and unshy for a while. Surely he wasn't bashful with his mother, for heaven's sake. My mother was still banging away on the lute and hadn't heard the doorbell.

"I'll get my mom," I said, sliding toward the stairs, but Mrs. Halibut shook her head.

"No need, Ivy dear. We're heading on home. We don't want to tire you out. Now, just let us know if you'd like to visit us sometime and we'll arrange it. Ah, *neighbors*, our first neighbors on our first block. You see that out there?" She pointed in the general direction of their yard. I nodded, even though I didn't know what she was pointing at. "That's our first tree."

"Oh," I said.

"It's the settled life for us. Tell your mother I will see her in church. And that I have decided to join the casserole committee and Lutes for Lent she told me about." With that, she shepherded a subdued Alfred out of the house.

Five

THAT EVENING I JOINED my parents for dinner downstairs. Naturally, I had to have pillows behind my back and an afghan wrapped around my knees.

"Don't spill spaghetti sauce on my best afghan," said my mother.

I dabbed delicately at my mouth. For my first dinner downstairs in over a month, one might have expected balloon bouquets, banners reading WELCOME BACK TO THE TABLE, IVY, or perhaps someone leaping out to videotape the moment. But no, no, it was business as usual.

"Interest rates, those little devils," said my father, gesturing with the Parmesan shaker until everything lay under a thin blanket of the first cheese fall of the year, "have risen. Ah, we'll see real-estate dealers take a bloodbath."

"No kidding," said my mother, one eye still on her afghan. I pointed to my father to indicate that he was the one who had shaken cheese on it.

"And now, my bedraggled daughter," he roared, giving me his complete and undivided attention. "How was your day?"

"I talked to the boy next door," I said.

"Splendid," said my father.

"Yes, Alfred came over and they had a nice chat, didn't you, dear? Did you two have anything in common?"

I thought hard. "I don't know," I said, unable to explain that having something in common somehow seemed beside the point.

I picked at my spaghetti.

"Ah, B.D., how it does my heart good to see you sitting at the table again, able to slurp up the pasta that is the life's blood of the Italian," said my father expansively.

"We're not Italian," I said. We are Scottish, in fact.

"Yes!" bellowed my father, not at all downstruck by this observation. "But we all have a little Italian blood in us, B.D. We all have a little Italian blood."

He finished slurping up the last spaghetti strand on his plate, smiled broadly, and then went into the kitchen and fixed himself a large bowl of ice cream with figs and wheat germ on it, which was his invariable dessert. If my mother made something like a cake, he put figs and wheat germ on *that*. You could count on my father. He was a man of habits.

After that, my father went to watch the news. Usually, both my parents watched the news while I loaded the dishwasher, but since I was still on the sick list I tumbled back into bed upstairs. I was happy to do so. It had been a very exciting day. I snuggled into my pillows. That certainly was a strange story about Alfred's mother's teeth.

A sudden chill went up my spine. *If* the Halibuts were in fact the Clanceys and if they *were* fictional, if *that* could be true, then maybe the tooth fairy was *real*. And if she was and Alfred put my old bicuspid under his pillow, maybe the tooth fairy *would* show up and jam a bunch of teeth into his mouth. And it would be all my fault.

My head was swimming. After so many days with nothing to think about, it was too much. I felt feverish again. I didn't know what was real and what wasn't.

I sat up in bed and looked over at his house. Then an even worse thought occurred to me. It was *my* tooth under the pillow over there. If there really was a tooth fairy she could probably tell whose tooth it had been and she might come over to *my* house and jam teeth into *me*. I raced downstairs and started putting on my boots and coat. My mother came in and said, "Ivy, what in the world do you think you're doing?"

"I have to go tell Alfred something right now. It's important," I said.

"Don't be ridiculous," said my mother, trying to grab my coat and yank it off.

"I have to get something back," I said, tightening it around me.

"You're being silly. Now stop this. What's so important that you have to go racing out in the cold at this hour?"

"I can't explain," I said.

My mother grabbed my sleeve, pulled me over, and felt my forehead. "Richard!" she called to my father. "You must have a fever again," she said.

My father came in, felt my forehead, and told my mother that in his opinion I didn't have a fever. "Go to bed, B.D. We'll see you in the morning."

I clomped upstairs. There must be some way to warn Alfred. What did Nancy Drew do in situations like this? Flash Morse Code signals with a flashlight, that's what. I went back downstairs.

"Ivy," said my mother. "What's wrong? Did you want some tapioca?"

It is pointless to try to explain to my mother that normal people occasionally think about other things.

"Do we have any books around the house with Morse Code?" I asked.

My parents looked at each other. "No," said my mother.

"Do you know any Morse Code?" I asked my father.

"No," said my father. "I can't say that I do, but I once learned the Dewey Decimal System."

I went upstairs. Then I had another idea. I got out

the flashlight and took a piece of paper and wrote on it in clear block letters DO NOT PUT THAT TOOTH UNDER YOUR PILLOW. I flashed the light at Alfred's window, hoping he would leap up, look out, and read the note. I flashed the light in dips and arcs. I tried to make the beam reach his window, but there is only so far a flashlight will flash. Surely he will eventually come to his window, I thought. A large looming figure did at last appear. It seemed to pause and stare out. Then Alfred's shade was snapped down and that was that. I thought it was extremely sinister that Alfred's mother closed his shade just as I was trying to reach him with urgent information.

I had been in such a lather that I hadn't heard my mother's furry little feet creep-creep-creeping up the stairs. When she entered my room I jumped and dropped everything. She picked up the note and read DO NOT PUT THAT TOOTH UNDER YOUR PILLOW.

"Well, I wondered when you would begin to want someone to play with," she said, smiling as if that was a good thing. "But really, Ivy, it is bedtime. I'll deliver this to Alfred in the morning if you like."

"No, that's okay," I said. I could hardly tell her it would be too late by then. Who would believe such a story? I went to bed with a heavy heart, wondering which one of us would awaken with a frightening smile.

All night long I kept waking up to feel around my mouth for extra teeth. The next morning was Sunday, and when I looked over, the Halibuts' car wasn't there. My mom said she would check for them at church.

Since I had gotten sick she went to church, while my dad stayed home with me. When she got home she said they hadn't been there either. I tapped my foot impatiently all day. Maybe they were gone forever. Maybe they had never been. On Monday morning, I dragged myself downstairs and found Mrs. Halibut with my mother and the casserole committee, throwing together industrial-sized casseroles for the shelter downtown. A couple of days a week, the casserole committee used our kitchen to mix together the contents of number-ten-sized tin cans of stuff. When my father was around, he would always drift in and taste raw casseroles, declaring them week after week the best he had ever had.

My mother felt my forehead again for fever. It was becoming quite a nervous twitch with her.

"So, how's Alfred this morning?" I asked Mrs. Halibut. "When you were gone yesterday I thought maybe you were seeing an emergency doctor or dentist or something."

"We had to drop Mr. Halibut off across the state. The circus had a publicity crisis and he had to rejoin them sooner than planned. But Alfred is excellent. Roaring with animal spirits. Never a prey to malaise, my boy."

The other women put down their cans to stare at Mrs. Halibut.

"Anything new going on with his mouth?" I asked casually.

"Same old mouth far as I know," sang Mrs. Halibut.

"Doesn't have any extra teeth, does he?" I said.

"Ivy, what are you getting at?" asked my mother.

"He *did* put a tooth under his pillow Saturday night, didn't he?" I demanded.

"Not that I know of. Hey, creamed corn!" Mrs. Halibut yelled to Mrs. May. Everyone stared at Mrs. Halibut politely but cooly. Mrs. May is ninety-four years old and everyone is so amazed that she can still heft those number-ten cans that they are willing to wait until she remembers it's her turn to pour in something.

Mrs. May said loudly, "Huh? OH YEAH," and dumped the creamed corn in. Mrs. May was almost totally deaf and had the hard-of-hearing habit of shouting at people.

Well, it looked like this tooth-fairy business was just so much nonsense, after all.

"Ivy dear, I don't know if you should be in here when we are making the church casseroles," said Mrs. Witherspoon. "You have been ill."

"She's not contagious," said my mother. "But go away anyway, Ivy."

"Oh, Ivy," said Mrs. Halibut, and reached into her pocket, extracted my tooth, and tossed it to me, "Alfred said to give this to you."

I went back to my room to try and piece things together. Had Alfred lied? Had his mother lied? Someone wasn't being very truthful. I got out my manuscript and read it thoroughly, looking for clues, but in my book Alfred wasn't even an Alfred, he was a Clarissa.

I was beginning to have my doubts that Alfred *was* fictional. But if he wasn't fictional, that was one whopper he had told about his mother and the tooth fairy. Why would he do that?

It was several hours and many bowls of tapioca later that afternoon that Alfred rang the doorbell. I knew it was him because I had been waiting hawk-like for him since school let out.

"Why, come in," I heard my mother say.

I put on my sweatsuit and minced my way downstairs.

My mother smiled and left us alone.

"Either you didn't put that tooth under your pillow or you made up everything about the tooth fairy or both," I said coldly.

"Here," said Alfred, "have a chocolate bar." He handed one to me. I would have declined, but who can resist a Milky Way?

"I have a confession to make," said Alfred.

"Yeah, me too," I said, deciding to throw mercy to the winds. "You're fictional."

"I'm *what?*" asked Alfred, tossing his mop out of his lasar-eyes.

"Not real," I said. "I wrote you. Here." I handed him my manuscript.

He sat on the couch and didn't look up until he had read all four chapters.

"This is a story about a family named Clancey with a daughter named Clarissa," he said.

"I think you recognize yourself," I said meaningly.

"This family works for the circus—my dad works for the circus. They move to a small town—we moved to a small town. The mother is big—my mother is big. The father is small—my father is small. Beyond that, there are no similarities. But from this you draw the conclusion that I'm fictional?"

"Now, don't get excited," I said. "Being a book character isn't the end of the world. Some of my favorite people are book characters."

"If I'm a book character, what am I doing here?"

"That's an interesting question," I said, leaning forward and putting my fingertips together to cover up that I had no idea whatsoever. "Very interesting, indeed."

"How high was that fever you ran?" asked Alfred.

"We won't speak of it again," I said. "Now, what is it you wanted to tell me?"

"I made up the story about my mother and her teeth," he said.

"Well, duh," I said, not wishing to let on that I had been duped.

"It was a pretty good story, wasn't it?" asked Alfred. "Of course, technically I was lying. I can see how one might think that, but I was really test-driving it."

"Test-driving it?" I asked.

Alfred went to his dripping winter coat and pulled out a scroll of papers from his pocket. "For my book," he said.

I could hardly form words. It was one thing to discover he was a fictional character, but a *writer?*

Six

"*WELL,*" *SAID ALFRED.* "Did you think you were the only writer in the world? One look at the library should tell you better."

"You're writing a book?" I asked, still open-mouthed. I sat down on the couch with a startled thump.

"That's right, and I wanted to put in a story about my mother's teeth but I wasn't sure if it would fly. It's a pretty incredible idea. However, you seem pretty smart and you bought it."

"Maybe I'm not as smart as I look," I said grimly.

"No," said Alfred. "I think you are. Anyhow, it worked, so I'm putting it in."

"You read my book, let me read yours," I said, reaching for it.

"No, I don't think so," said Alfred, pulling it back and rolling it up into its original scrunched-up mess. What kind of writer treats his manuscript with such irreverence?

"Well, anyhow, I was going to use the teeth story for *my* next chapter," I said.

"Use it how?" asked Alfred, sitting down, pushing his hair out of his eyes, and staring at me.

"I don't know," I said. "But I'm sure, given time, it would come to me."

"Ah. Well, I know exactly how I plan to use it," said Alfred.

"How?" I asked.

"I can't tell you, because I don't like to talk about a work in progress," said Alfred.

"Now, listen," I began, when my mother came in.

"Ovaltine?" she asked.

"No!" shouted both Alfred and myself.

My mother said, "Oh my," and went upstairs, from whence came the gentle toodle of the lute.

"Anyhow," said Alfred, "maybe you're the fictional one. Did it ever occur to you that you might be in *my* book?"

"No, it did not," I said firmly. "Because I am me and I remember always being me."

"Well, I remember always being me, too. I distinctly remember not being anyone else. I refuse to discuss this silly notion that we are all just book characters that you wrote. And the tooth-fairy story is mine and I am going right home to write it. I was going to tell you about my first day at school but now I'm not. Here's your homework. Which I will bring to you despite it all."

He went back to stand by the the door and I sulked. If I couldn't write about him and his family I would have to begin a whole new book. "All right," I said finally. "Keep the tooth-fairy story. I am sorry you don't want to tell me about your first day at school, but why you think I am going to be thrilled about getting homework I don't know. And I will start a new book, but you don't get to use everything that happens to us. I get at least every other real-life experience to turn into stories. And you'd better keep to the bargain, because I refuse to be friends with someone who haggles over every story."

"All right, but you know the tooth-fairy story was something I made up to begin with," said Alfred.

"You're haggling," I warned.

"See you tomorrow," said Alfred and marched out.

Hmmm, I thought, picking up a clean notebook to start a new manuscript. Maybe he wasn't fictional after all.

For the last two weeks of March, Alfred brought me my homework and picked it up the next day to deliver to school. He could not bring me any bits of gossip, as he didn't know anyone very well yet and, as he put it, kept himself to himself.

Finally I began to hear spring. Robins made an incredible din every morning. Dr. Nipon came over and pronounced me out of danger and ready to return to school. The next morning I got up and walked with Alfred.

"So, when am I going to meet your father?" I asked as we kicked a pebble down the street through the last remaining slush. We had become quite chummy, although we had never kicked a pebble together before. I had forgiven him his little lie about the tooth fairy and he had forgiven me for thinking him fictional (although privately the vote was not yet in on that one and I still kept a sharp lookout for clues).

"Oh, eventually," said Alfred. "He's still traveling. But," he practically shouted, as if suddenly remembering something, "Elmira Degoochy is coming for dinner tonight. She's the snake lady. Maybe you could come for dinner, too, and meet her."

"Really?" I said, getting out my notebook. I still didn't have a handle on a new book but a story about a snake lady seemed full of promise. "What did you say her name was again?"

"Elmira Degoochy," said Alfred. "I'll have to ask my mom."

I wrote it down. "Sounds good. And we are agreed that anything that we find out about her, I get to use for my book, right?"

"I wasn't thinking of her as book material," said Alfred.

"Everything is book material," said I. "Yes, I'd say it was about time I came over to your house. If my mother will let me, which I believe she will. Lately I've had the impression that if I didn't get better soon she was going to send me for one of those Arizona rest cures."

"What Arizona rest cures?" asked Alfred.

"Oh, I don't know," I said vaguely. "Or maybe the Swiss Alps. Like Heidi."

"You mean like Clara in *Heidi?*"

"I had better learn to yodel," I said. "Anyhow, she's a very nice Mom, but sometimes I feel she is missing an essential television-mom quality."

"You keep saying that," pointed out Alfred. "And I keep telling you that we've never owned a television."

"Well, jeez, what kind of cheesy circus was it you traveled with, anyway?" I asked.

"Why," asked Alfred slowly in what I knew was his edge-of-being-mad voice, "would you need a television if you could watch a three-ring circus every night, anyhow?"

We reached school and went to our classroom.

"Hello, Ivy," said Mrs. Cunningham, smiling. "How nice to see you back."

"Thank you, Mrs. Cunningham," I said. "Nice to be back." And I took my seat.

When I got home, I was tired.

"How was school?" my mother asked.

"Could have been worse," I said. "I hope I have not overdone it."

"Dr. Nipon said you were fit as a fiddle," said my mother.

"Pneumonia is one of those things you can get more than once," I pointed out cheerfully.

"You look okay to me," said my mother, who was making dinner.

"I'm sure you're right," I said. "Can I have dinner at Alfred's house? I know you're worried about me because it's already been a busy day and you would just die if I got sick like that again but I think I can do it."

"Fine," said my mother. "If you don't mind missing corned-beef-and-cabbage night."

"You can't have everything," I said and took some cookies upstairs. I got out my binoculars to see if the snake lady had made her appearance yet, but it was hard to tell. Mrs. Halibut had taken to pulling down quite a few of the shades lately.

Alfred phoned to say it was okay and to come on over, so I washed my face and put my notebook and pen in the back pocket of my jeans. I wasn't going to sit and write a novel at the dinner table. I had better manners than *that,* but a writer must be prepared to take a few surreptitious notes now and then. With Alfred a writer, too, they were probably used to it.

"Goodbye, dear. Have fun," called my mom.

"Don't stay too late, B.D.," said my father.

"I'll leave if I feel sick," I assured him.

"Good," said my parents and went back to their corned beef.

I knocked on the Halibuts' door and Mrs. Halibut answered. "Darling child," she exclaimed as she ushered me in. "I am so glad to see you returned to the land of the living. Welcome to our humble home."

Humble it might be, but it certainly didn't lack for color. Purple and yellow and green and red furniture was everywhere. The rooms were papered in candy-striped wallpaper of various bright hues. It did look like a circus tent.

Alfred sat in the living room with a glass of ginger ale in his hand. By his chair stood a woman whose first sweet youth was behind her. She had long tangled black hair, tattoos on her arms, and several teeth gone to meet their maker. So far, two-thirds of the people I had met from the circus had strange teeth. I wanted desperately to get out my notebook and make a note of this.

"Just a second, I dropped something outside," I said and ran outside to make a quick note, then ran back inside.

Mrs. Halibut pretended that I had never left the room. "Elmira dear, this is Alfred's friend, Ivy." I extended my hand and Elmira put down her glass to shake it. I emitted a little shriek. I hadn't meant to and it was embarrassing but her hand was cold and wet and my first unformed thought had been that it was that way from handling snakes. Fortunately, Elmira didn't know why I had shrieked.

"Oh, my goodness, I've been holding that icy glass," she said, wiping her hand off on her dress. "My hand must be freezing."

"It was a surprise," I said and sat down with a thump. As the grownups stayed standing, I felt more and more awkward. Should I stand again?

"This is our first dinner party," said Mrs. Halibut, smiling congenially upon us. "Can I get you a drink, Ivy?"

"Your first dinner party? What nonsense, Georgina," said Elmira. "What about all those times we used to get everyone together after the shows?"

"I wasn't counting sharing a bucket from Hasty Chicken," said Mrs. Halibut. "Lovely though those occasions were. You see, Elmira, now that we are town folk, we are rejoicing in town ways: dinner parties, neighbors, friends of a permanent nature. We have a tree."

"So you wrote," said Elmira. "A real live tree."

"I assure you it's quite real—branches, leaves, the whole nine yards."

"Can you beat that," said Elmira and finally sat down.

"So, what will you have?" asked Mrs. Halibut again. I asked for a ginger ale since Alfred was drinking it and no one had presented me with any other choices.

Mrs. Halibut left to get my drink, and the snake lady, Alfred, and I sat smiling at each other, each of our brains, I'm sure, scrambling like rats in mazes looking for some topic of conversation to fill the silence.

"So," I said at last, resourceful to the end, "how are your snakes?"

"Peachy," said the snake lady.

She laughed politely. Alfred laughed politely. I laughed politely. The ball, as far as I was concerned, was in their court.

"Say, I like this town of yours," said the snake lady finally. "Seems like a nice place. Nice town hall."

"Oh, the best." I nodded.

Mrs. Halibut came back and handed me my drink.

"Nice school."

"We have several," I pointed out.

"Churches," said the snake lady.

"Lots," I agreed. Oh, the conversation was coming hard and fast now.

"Houses."

"We gave up huts a long time ago," I said, nodding.

"Sort of an ideal existence," said the snake lady.

"Paradise" I agreed. Then, deciding I should keep a record of this conversation, especially that witty remark about the huts, I excused myself to the bathroom and wrote it all down.

When I returned, Mrs. Halibut, who was sitting down draining her drink, said "Dinner" and then sprang back onto those long grasshopper legs. In fact, the more I thought about it, the more I thought that Mrs. Halibut looked exactly like a grasshopper. This occasioned another trip to the bathroom.

When I came back, we shuffled into the dining room. It was orange. The table was yellow.

"Now, peops," said Mrs. Halibut as, heavily burdened with an assortment of tureens and platters, she maneuvered her way to the table, "I'm just learning to cook, so I don't know as I know what's what yet, but I hope it's at least edible."

I'm not sure what I was expecting, Mrs. Halibut being a new cook and all. I figured some variation of the church casseroles she had learned to prepare, which would have been just fine with me. What I got instead was my first introduction to courses. I have naturally eaten more than one thing at a meal before, but my mother always puts everything on the table at the same time, so that, for instance, if you like to vary your salad experience with, say, a little bite of meat loaf, why, you can do it. Mrs. Halibut started us off with turtle soup. It was a true test of my savoir-faire. I kept one eye on the tureen at all times, waiting for a couple of eyes to poke out, but thank goodness they did not. It was not at all helpful of Elmira to tell us which snakes ate turtles and which didn't. After that, we moved on to a plate with two raviolis. This was alarming for three reasons. First, because I thought this was the main course and I wanted to leap up and cry, "Now, Mrs. Halibut, let us not be niggling!" Secondly, because the sauce was *under* the ravioli and I just couldn't figure that one out at all. What was the point of sauce if it was on the *plate?* For a grand finale, were we supposed to eat the china? That would certainly be spectacular. And thirdly because the sauce, when tasted, turned out to be raspberry. I watched Mrs. Halibut's face, waiting for the terrible moment when she realized she had put spaghetti sauce on the cheesecake and raspberry sauce on the ravioli, but as she chomped delightedly away I realized this pleasure was to be denied me. And so dinner continued to the main course, which was enlivened by little bundles of vegetables gift-wrapped in green onions. I opened mine excitedly, thinking there might be a prize inside, but all there was was more vegetables. The main course itself was wrapped, too—this time in parchment paper. I never did figure out what it was exactly and from the look on Elmira's and Alfred's face this was a secret Mrs. Halibut would carry to her grave. It must have been a lot of work, tying everything up like that. It certainly was a lot of work untying everything. I could see why grownup dinner parties took so long. But we were all very polite about it. Especially me.

"It's not much, but I made it myself," said Mrs. Halibut, clearing away the remains of things in perhaps a tad too much raspberry vinegar.

"It was lovely," said Elmira, parchment paper from the mysterious main course still clinging to her teeth.

"Well, I tried," said Mrs. Halibut. "I got the ideas from magazines. Now, what should we do? What do people do after dinner parties?"

Mrs. Halibut turned to me. I didn't know, as frankly this was the first dinner party I had ever been invited to. I was trying desperately to memorize everything we had eaten and everything the snake lady had said, so I excused myself to the bathroom again to make my notes. I was just coming into the living room when I heard Mrs. Halibut saying, "Well, she's been sick for some time," and I realized I had better stop making these urgent trips to take notes. I was almost too embarrassed to return, but I reminded myself that writers have to be tough and single-minded.

"So, dear," said Mrs. Halibut, smiling at me kindly. Only, now that I had decided that she looked like a grasshopper it made me feel like a small and tasty bug. "What is it people do after dinner parties?"

"Games!" I said. I do not know how this came to me, but we moved the furniture around and I taught them charades, dictionary, and musical chairs.

"You're making this up," whispered Alfred in my ear as we went round and round the remaining chair to the stirring rendition of Pop Goes the Weasel I was humming and the shrieks of joy from Mrs. Halibut and the snake lady, who seemed to have really taken to this party game.

"I swear to you I'm not," I whispered back and then yelled "Aha!" as I stopped humming and grabbed the remaining chair.

"Wouldn't it be more fair if the music came from a non-player?" asked Alfred.

"No, it's always played this way," I lied.

"Well, gosheroony, it's nine o'clock," said Mrs. Halibut rather pointedly, so I took my leave.

I was lying in bed thinking about the whole evening when I realized that I had it all written down. I got out my notes and reread them and fell asleep imagining that everyone really looked like some kind of bug if you stopped to think about it.

$\mathcal{S}$even

THE VERY NEXT DAY the snake lady bought the
house across the street from the Halibuts'. I could see
now that this business about ideal existence had been
more than polite conversation. Mrs. Halibut was delighted to have an old friend so close at hand. Probably, when you have spent the morning with the ladies'
knitting circle at church, it is a relief to have someone
with whom you can discuss tattoos. Alfred was happy,
too. He missed the circus.

"They could write to you," I pointed out while copying down another tombstone name. We were at the
cemetery, where I was trying to find interesting names
for the characters in my new book which I was trying
unsuccessfully to write. I had thrown out about fourteen false starts at last count, including stories about

the snake lady which never went anywhere at all. Alfred said he was bogged down in his book, too. "Mathilde Dapswinkle," I read. "Horace Whippensnoop. Prunella Sharksnapper. Anyhow, if you like the circus life so much, why don't you write about *that*? Gosh, how many people have had the golden opportunity to live with a circus? I bet it would make a pretty good book."

"Maybe," said Alfred, sitting gloomily on a tomb and wiping the hair out of his eyes. Now that we knew each other better, he often let me see his eyes. "But you know very well you can't just say, I think I will write a book about the circus. That's not how books happen."

"True enough," I muttered bitterly.

"Anyhow," said Alfred, "this Saturday night my mom is going to have a welcome-to-town party for the snake lady. She's inviting Lutes for Lent and the casserole committee and everyone she can think of and your family is invited. She is asking everyone to bring something to eat, so she can figure out what people around here like."

"A word to the wise, less arugula and more Jell-O," I said, writing down Myrtle Mavisbine.

Little crocuses covered Myrtle Mavisbine's grave. It was quite pretty in a macabre way. "Myrtle Mavisbine, Myrtle Mavisbine . . . is there a story there? Nothing."

"Why don't you write about your own life?" asked Alfred, hitching up an eyebrow—a friendly facial habit of his that I kind of liked.

"Nah, dull as dishwater," I said.

"Come on, let's go home," said Alfred, pulling his jacket tightly around him. It had started to rain.

That night at dinner I told my parents about the party.

"Splendid, splendid," said my dad. "I wonder where Ms. Degoochy plans to bank?"

"I wonder what kind of job she will get," said my mother, passing round the peas and carrots. "I mean, there's hardly going to be an opening for a snake lady here, and from Alfred's mother's account, she's not at retirement age. She'll have to do something for a living."

"She's hoping to open a snake kennel," I said through a mouthful of pot roast.

"Close your mouth, dear, when you're eating," said my mother. "What's a snake kennel?"

"You know, it's like a dog kennel, a place for people to board their snakes when they're on vacation."

"I had no idea that so many people kept snakes for pets," said my father. "Fascinating."

"Hmm," said my mother.

By the time party night came there was already a buzz about the snake lady. I heard my mother telling my father about it as they were getting dressed. My mom had made a mountain of that mixed cereal and pretzel and peanuts stuff to take over.

"There's a lot of whispering about 'the circus coming to town' and 'letting just anyone join committees,' etc." said my mother.

"I thought that was the point of a church group," said my father. "Just anyone can join."

"Well, of course," said my mother. "That's just it. They're all being such stinkers. They've been nice to Georgina because *I* brought her in, but now that Georgina wants to bring the snake lady in, there's been a lot of gossip. I'm sure I only see the tip of the iceberg, too. I just hope they don't do something as mean-spirited as boycotting this party."

"Ah well, everyone likes a party, and perhaps when they see how good she is with her snakes, the talk will die down. Interesting profession to go into. Can't wait to talk to her," said my father.

Despite my mother's worries, everyone who had been invited to the party came. It was a mob. Food was piled high in the kitchen and spread out over the sideboard and dining-room table. I noted there was a disproportionate number of lime Jell-O salads.

"I told you so," I said to Alfred, pointing to a quivering green mass. Alfred was supposed to be welcoming people, but he had his hair combed intentionally over his eyes and he kept to dark corners as much as possible. I stayed with him a good deal to compare notes but also drifted about in the crowd. "Listen," I hissed as I dragged him along on one of my forays. "You can't be a good writer if you don't get out there and hear how people talk."

"I know how people talk, thank you very much," said Alfred. "And it's one of the reasons I am going back to my corner."

Elmira was the last to come and her entrance was spectacular. She arrived with a snake on her head. One could perhaps overlook the spangled harem costume, the seventeen gold chains, the long, long dangling gold earrings, the livid orange lipstick and purple eye shadow, but it was pretty hard to overlook something coiled and rattling. There were several shrieks from the faint of heart. Elmira fortunately seemed to be oblivious to it all and went about happily partaking of Jell-O in its many guises and asking children if they could reach up and give the snake a stuffed egg. She was a real hit among the younger crowd. I went over to sit with Alfred, who was growing increasingly gloomier.

"Oh, cheer up, it's not *your* fault," I said. We watched my father rush up and begin an animated conversation with the snake lady. He was perfectly delighted that she had brought a snake and kept feeding it little tidbits off his plate as they talked.

"People are saying things about her, I can tell," said Alfred. "And after that they are going to say things about my family."

"Nonsense," I said. "Let them try. They'd have me to deal with. People always like to gossip and they'll be grateful that they now have something really strange to talk about. And we'll just refuse to be intimidated."

"I'm already intimidated," said Alfred.

"No, you're not," I said. "Next month is the big bake-off at the church and you and I are going to enter

it together and we're going to make the snake lady
enter it, too. And your mom, too."

"I can't bake," said Alfred.

"Neither can I," I said. "Who cares? We can learn
and we can enter same as anyone else."

"What good do you think it's going to do?" asked
Alfred.

"Why, it will show everyone that they can't squelch
us so easily, no siree. After all, it's our town, too."

"You're right," said a lady in front of us, turning
around and nodding fervently in agreement. "Who
needs such things in town!" Then she doddered off. It
just goes to show you that people will hear what they
want to hear.

"You see," said Alfred. "You see what we're up
against? You just want something to do because you
can't think of a story to write."

"Hmm, it might make a story," I said with interest.
"But that's not why I suggested it."

"I do not want to go to war with a whole community," said Alfred, stubbornly hunching his shoulders
and looking as if he wanted to turn himself inside out.

"Who said anything about a war, silly?" I asked.
"All we're going to do is bake a cake."

Alfred flicked his hair out of his eyes long enough
for me to see a look of skeptical reproach. This had no
effect, because I was sure that as usual I was right.

Eight

THE NEXT DAY Mrs. Halibut, Alfred, and I went to the snake lady's for tea. Elmira Degoochy met us at the door in another interesting tummy-revealing outfit.

"Do you know, Georgina," she said to Alfred's mom as she graciously led us around the house, "that there's a store in town where you can get furniture for a song. Just a song. Of course, some of the couches and whatnot are missing their stuffing, but aren't we all? Ivy dear, watch the cobra," she said as I almost tripped over it. "And it is so nice to finally live somewhere where my snakies can roam about."

"Don't you think you ought to keep them in cages?" asked Alfred.

"Alfred," said Mrs. Halibut. "We do not second-guess grownups."

"It's all right, Georgina. I'm not a grownup. I'm Auntie Elmira the snake lady. Born free!" sang Elmira and almost stepped on one of the snakes herself. She led us to a battered kitchen set, where she had put out tea and cake. It was delicious cake. "Snake cake," she said when I commented on it.

"So you already know how to bake," I said.

"Well, of course, Ivy dear, do you think I was *born* in the circus?" She tittered and then stopped in embarrassment because of course Alfred *had* been born in the circus. She cleared her throat. "You know, Georgina, I think that party went very well. I think they all accepted me and drew me to their bosom. I have always wanted to be drawn to a town's bosom."

"Hem, yes," said Mrs. Halibut.

"And already I love it here. I am building my snake kennel in the workshop out back. And, Georgina dear, I, too, have a tree!" She smiled serenely and batted her false eyelashes over the teacup.

"That's nice," said Mrs. Halibut and tried batting her eyelashes, too, only hers weren't false, so she didn't get the same effect.

"Oh, a town of my own! Friends! Neighbors! Libraries! You know, tomorrow I am going to march right down and get memberships everywhere. A membership at the Y (you will do laps with me, won't you, dear?), a membership at the library, a membership with the automobile association."

"Do you have a car?" asked Mrs. Halibut.

"Do you think they are going to insist upon that?"

asked Elmira. "Memberships in everything. And I'm going to volunteer just as soon as I get my business set up. I'm going to candy-stripe and Brownie-lead and join the PTA!"

"Don't you have to be a parent or a teacher for that?" asked Alfred.

"Maybe in some towns, but not in *my* town," said Elmira dizzyingly.

I was worried. It looked like Elmira really did think she had found some sort of heaven on earth. Which she certainly hadn't. At most, we're just ordinary schlubs around here. I never would have expected the snake lady to have a side like this. She certainly didn't look like a joiner. Alfred had told me that she lived for those snakes. I guess if you're the devoted type, when let loose, you just go around and devote yourself to pieces.

"There's a bake-off next month at the church," I said to Elmira. "Alfred and I are going to make a cake. Why don't you enter your snake cake?"

"Ah, you see, you see," said the snake lady, clasping her hands ecstatically. "Life is too full!"

The next two Mondays after school I met with Alfred in my kitchen. My mother didn't mind us experimenting as long as we cleaned up after ourselves.

"Now," I began, getting down a stack of cookbooks, "for the perfect recipe."

"What's wrong with the chocolate cake we made last Monday?" asked Alfred, who didn't seem to get the point *at all*.

"Don't you want to *win?*" I asked, madly flipping through pages. "Then we gotta find out who is judging this thing and what he or she likes. The judge can't help but be prejudiced by what he likes. After all, if his favorite dessert is prune pie and he hates icing, then there's no point making a cake, is there?"

"I guess not," said Alfred, yawning.

"Wake up!" I shouted.

Then I had an idea. "Come on," I said, grabbing Alfred.

"Where are we going?" he asked, trooping behind me.

"Mom! Mom!" I called. She was upstairs perfecting her lute. One might, if one were less charitable, call her obsessed. She had gotten so good on it that she could play complicated classical stuff and her fingers moved so quickly you could practically see sparks on the strings. As we watched, she worked feverishly, going faster and faster.

"Bach," I whispered to Alfred. We waited politely until the piece came to a crashing halt. Then Mom came back to earth and said, "Yes, dear?"

"Who's judging the bake-off this year?" I asked.

"The bake-off?" Mom asked.

"The bake-off!" I shouted.

"Ah yes, the bake-off. Ah . . . Reverend Dwindle, of course. He's never judged one and they're running out of impartial observers."

"I'm surprised it took them this long to ask him," I

said. "He seems like the first person they would ask."

"Well, yes," said my mother. "But you know how these contests go, he thought warring factions in the church might claim he had chosen the winning cake because he is in league with the garage sale for new choir pews, as opposed to the raffle for the baptismal font."

"Then why don't people submit their baked goods anonymously?" Alfred asked from beneath the hair.

"Well," said my mother, smiling at him kindly. She always smiles at him kindly because she is so grateful that I have finally found someone I like. I hate to think what it will be like if I ever decide to get married. "You see *that* wouldn't be any fun at all because people want to have their names on their masterpieces so people can ooh and aaah and say, 'Oh, that Mrs. Jones's strawberry pie! Why don't my berries ever glisten like that?' and 'There's Mrs. Joad's entry. Tsk-tsk.'"

"Come on," I said. "Let's go over to Reverend Dwindle's office."

We were going to bike over to Reverend Dwindle's office, but it turned out that Alfred didn't have a bike. If you have never lived in one place before, there are a lot of things you don't realize you need. Fortunately, Alfred knew how to ride a bike, because the clowns in the circus had taught him. Alfred was going to have to get one, but it was one of those soft spring days where the only thing better than walking would be flying, so I didn't mind. Reverend Dwindle's secretary winked at us when we came in. I guess if you are a church secre-

tary you had better like everyone, even kids. She sent
us into Reverend Dwindle's office, where he was shuf-
fling papers around his desk.

"So," said Reverend Dwindle. "What can I do for
you?"

He had one of those rich baritones that always
sound as if the owner is about to burst into song. It
should have made him seem jolly but it didn't, because
he always looked worried, as if he wasn't sure he was
doing the right thing. I have had teachers like this.
Nice women whom you felt sorry for by the time the
class got through with them. If you look like you're not
sure you should be in charge, others quickly come to
the conclusion that indeed you shouldn't, and they
usually find a swift solution. But I liked Reverend
Dwindle. He kept his sermons short, especially in
good weather, and he was polite to everyone, even
us.

"How about this bake-off?" I asked. "We hear you
are judging it. I had this idea to ask you what desserts
you like and don't like, cause I figure if we make something you hate, then you can't be impartial about it
even though you might try. I mean, it's not like you're
a professional taster or something. You're bound to be
influenced by your preferences."

He listened frowning and then got up and got some
blank paper and wrote something. I hate it when people take action without explaining what they are doing.
The natural thing is to respond first. But we waited pa-

tiently for him to finish. Alfred, I noted, hadn't come out of his hair once. You can never tell who is going to especially intimidate Alfred.

"There," said Reverend Dwindle. "Pin this on the church bulletin board on your way out, if you will. I think you're right, but we had better allow everyone to have the information in order to be perfectly fair."

I read what he handed me. "I do not wish to influence anyone's choice of entry for the bake-off, but I cannot abide puddings of any sort. I am especially fond of cakes and pies, with the exception of cream pies (too much like puddings), and I don't much like things with fruit hidden in them."

"Are you certain this is absolutely all?" I asked. I wanted to make sure we didn't prepare something he forgot he hated, but he nodded solemnly.

We thanked him and walked down the halls, which had a holy used-candle smell.

"You'd think someone rejoicing in the Lord would smile a bit more," said Alfred as we pinned the notice on the board.

"He smiles," I said. "But it's always one of those costume smiles like he is smiling because he thinks he ought to. I guess if you're a preacher you worry a lot about doing the right thing and people who worry a lot don't smile very well."

We walked home. "Listen, Alfred, why don't you have supper at our house? My mom bumped the casserole committee from this morning to tonight, and whenever she does that, my dad and I have to fend for ourselves at dinner. We could make sandwiches and eat them on trays in front of the TV."

Alfred had a lot of TV watching to catch up on.

"We ought to be thinking of a good dessert to make," he said. He sure did have an earnest streak about him. Still, I admired it.

"No problem. He likes cakes. He likes pie."

"Yes, but did you notice he didn't say what he especially likes? Just what he doesn't like. So we're back to guessing."

"By gosh, you're right," I said. Always under the hair thinking, that guy. "Oh well." Really, it had been a long day. I just wanted my sandwiches and TV at this point.

When we got in the front hall, we could smell the casseroles being mixed. There was a browning hamburger-and-onion smell that went straight to my heart.

"Come on," I said, pulling a shy and reluctant Alfred toward the kitchen. We had just gotten there when Elmira burst in our back door and plopped several rutabagas on the kitchen table.

"Look what I've discovered," she said.

All the ladies looked at her rather coldly and Mrs. Johnson, the most reptilian of all, said, "They're rutabagas," in a toneless voice.

"Yes, I know," squealed Elmira happily. "I now know why God made man!"

There was a long silence after this. No one was even

polite enough to change the subject. Finally Mrs. May said, "WHY?" in her awful old creaky voice.

"So there would be someone to eat the rutabagas!" said Elmira.

Everyone rolled her eyes or looked away or shuffled about doing unnecessary things with gravy.

"STOP TALKING ABOUT GOD," yelled Mrs. May. "YOU'RE MAKING EVERYONE NERVOUS."

But Elmira was unquenchable. "Have you ever eaten the little darlings?" she asked, looking around and holding rutabagas under several flinching noses. "Have you? They're marvelous. They're more than marvelous. They're miraculous. You know I have traveled with the circus for years and years and years and years and now I have so many vegetables to catch up on. So I brought some for the casserole," she said, smiling and batting her false eyelashes at everyone.

"Everyone knows about rutabagas." Mrs. Meyer sniffed.

"We don't put vegetables in our casseroles," said Mrs. Johnson. I never liked Mrs. Johnson. She reminded me of a floor mop.

"What about creamed corn?" I asked. I couldn't bear to see them deflate Elmira. It was exciting to see *anybody* so excited about *anything*. I didn't see why the ladies couldn't just say something polite like, oh yes, weren't rutabagas grand. Alfred had left the kitchen. I saw him sitting on the couch, nervously tapping a foot.

"And frozen mixed vegetables, you put those in," I said, gathering steam.

"Ivy dear," began my mother warningly. I could tell she felt like I did or she would have shut me up more effectively.

"And onions, *there's* a root vegetable. Potatoes, too," I said.

"Ivy, really," said my mother.

"Ivy, I had no idea you paid so much attention to our recipes," said Mrs. Johnson in tones that made everyone even more uncomfortable. She picked up the rutabagas firmly and put them out of the way on top of our bread box. "Now, let's see, whose turn is it?" she asked, looking down at the recipe and the line of women hefting number-ten tin cans.

"Here," said my mother, surrendering her skillet of hamburger to Elmira. "You put this in when it is your turn. I must speak to Ivy."

She went into the hall with me.

"Poor Elmira," I hissed.

"Yes, I know," said my mother. "But you don't make things better by antagonizing Mrs. Johnson."

"Sorry. Listen, can Alfred and I make sandwiches for our supper and have them in front of the TV?"

"Certainly, if you can do it without getting in everyone's way," said my mother.

I went back to the crowded kitchen and deliberately got the rutabagas off the bread box.

"Creamed corn, shake a leg!" yelled Mrs. Halibut.

"WHAT?" asked Mrs. May. "HAVEN'T I ALREADY PUT IT IN?"

"Look in the can," said Elmira helpfully. "That's what I would do. If it's still in the can, then it's not in the casserole."

"OH," said Mrs. May, looking down and frowning, then grumpily tossing it in. She didn't acknowledge this helpful hint, but as she was pretty grumpy all the time, it was hard to tell if it had irked her.

"What are you doing?" asked my mother as I got out the carving board and a knife and began to slice the rutabagas.

"Making rutabaga sandwiches. How I *love* rutabaga sandwiches," I said. Elmira smiled happily, but the other women just looked stonily away. I made two rutabaga sandwiches and a couple of p.b. and j.'s. My father came in and beamed at the gathering. He lifted a rutabaga sandwich half off my plate and bit into it, oblivious to the political climate. "Delicious, simply delicious!" he said. "What do you call this, Ivy?"

"Rutabaga," I said.

"Make me a couple more, will you?" he asked. Then he got a fork and stuck it in the casserole. "Best I ever tasted, ladies," he said and sailed happily out.

I took a tentative bite of the rutabaga sandwich to see if I had unwittingly discovered something, but my advice about rutabaga sandwiches is, don't. I delivered the ones I had made to my dad and then took the p.b. and j.'s into the TV room for Alfred and myself. Alfred sat quietly and ate his sandwich. He looked worried.

"Alfred, no matter what happens, you will be my

best friend," I said. Actually, he was my only friend, but I didn't think it necessary to point that out.

Alfred flicked his hair out of his face and gave me a penetrating look with those eyes of his. "So you think something will happen, do you?" he asked.

Nine

WELL, OF COURSE more things *did* happen, because something else always happens, or else, I guess, you're dead. Most of the things that happened were just ordinary things like more school and the inevitable spelling tests, but on the extraordinary side of things there was Elmira and her snakes. She made leashes for them and started to take them for walks. I admit it was a little creepy to see them slither past as you went down the street, but after all, if you weren't used to dogs it would be pretty creepy to see these hairy quadrupeds brush past you on leashes, not to mention the fact that they always seem to want to sniff you and bark and stuff. I am not a dog fan myself. They drool. Snakes may drool, too, for all I know, but if they do, they are so close to the ground that it isn't much noticeable. Anyhow, Elmira started to get a reputation. That's how it is in a small town sometimes. Not to know you is not to like you. Elmira was finding it hard to volunteer for stuff, according to Mrs. Halibut. When Elmira went down to be a Brownie leader, they told her that first she had to have a Brownie of her own at home. The PTA said she could come to the meetings but they discouraged it. They said she was civic-minded but misguided and next time not to bring her snake. It didn't seem to deflate her at all, though, so happy was she to be in Springfield. She started to plant a garden, instead.

I heaved a sigh of relief for Alfred's sake. I thought as long as Elmira was busy among the petunias maybe the tide of public opinion would seep out gently and Alfred could just fade into the woodwork again, which is all he really wanted. Then the Gambinis moved in.

Alfred arrived at our house one sunny Saturday morning with the news. My mom, dad, and I were in the kitchen, eating French toast. My father had made an enormous platter of it. He just loves making it. He gets carried away breaking the eggs, dipping the bread, flipping the stuff around, and putting on powdered sugar with a sieve. It's very good French toast but we always wind up throwing away a pile of it at the end of the day. Once, when I pointed this out to my mother, she said, "Everyone should have a hobby." Well, if she didn't care, I didn't, but she wasn't going to get the thrifty-homemaker award. My father was delighted to see Alfred. In part because he likes "that thing that lives under the hair," as he refers to him, and partly because it was an excuse to make yet more French toast.

Alfred ate quietly under his hair until my parents took themselves off and then he flicked it impatiently away and said, "The Gambinis are coming to town."

I thought about this. I was hip. I could play along. "Are they going to break our legs with tire irons?" I whispered in a frightened, conspiratorial way.

Alfred looked at me searchingly and then rolled his eyes. "Now listen, Ivy, this isn't a game. The *Flying* Gambinis."

"Oh, more circus people," I said, finishing chewing and feeling like throwing up, as I did every Saturday morning.

"Right. More circus people," said Alfred.

"Well, don't look so worried," I said. "These are your friends, right? They can't all be as peculiar as the snake lady."

"It's not a matter of being peculiar," said Alfred. "No one wants any circus people around and you know it."

"Oh, don't be so gloomy," I said.

"It doesn't do any good to pretend not to know what's going on, Ivy. I know *you* don't feel that way, but let us take, for example, birthday parties. How many have I been invited to since moving here? None, that's how many."

"So what?" I said. "I haven't been invited to any, either. Unless people are inviting everyone in sight, I never get invited. But that's because I don't want to be. I am not a people person. However, if it's birthday parties you aspire to, you might consider coming out from under that hair occasionally."

"All right, leave the birthday parties out of it. You know if it wasn't for your mother, my mother and Elmira would never be allowed on the casserole committee. I can see a mob gathering and it won't be long before we are all run out of town on rails."

I didn't deny this. That was exactly the unwholesome type of thing I envisioned happening, too.

"Well, listen," I said finally. "Maybe we can help the Gambinis get settled in a more realistic way than we did the snake lady. We could explain to them that it would help if for a while they could act ordinary, so that people could see that not all circus people are strange. Not that *you're* strange. Although your mother kind of sticks out . . ."

"My mother is extremely ordinary," said Alfred coldly. "She is merely large . . . and a bit toothy."

"Sure, sure," I said, sighing. "And I'm sure the Gambinis are ordinary, too, in their own way. We're all ordinary in our own way. It's just that everybody's way of being ordinary is different. Can we get our bikes now?" Then I stopped, remembering Alfred's bikeless state. "Listen, Alfred, you're going to have to get your mother to buy you a bike."

"I don't like to ask," said Alfred gloomily. "We had hot dogs and beans for dinner three times this week."

"That's dreadful. You need your green vegetables,"

I said. I sometimes had to point this out to my mother, too. She hates to clean vegetables.

"I think we're having them because they are cheap. I think my dad hasn't flown back for a visit yet because we can't afford it," said Alfred.

"Well, gosh, you can get bikes at garage sales for a song. I only paid ten bucks for mine. I'll crack open my piggy bank. I've got at least ten bucks in there."

"You can't do that," said Alfred.

"Anything's better than having a friend in despair," I said.

"The Gambinis have bought a farm out on county road X," said Alfred.

"We can't walk all the way out there," I said. "You better ride on my handlebars. I knew I should have gotten one of those silly-looking banana-seat bikes. You could have ridden on the back behind me. Oh, well."

"It doesn't sound very safe to me," said Alfred.

I could have pointed out that it was safer than being run out of town, but I controlled myself.

It took many tumbling attempts to get him on the handlebars. Even though he was smaller than I was, he was no lightweight, and I found steering the darn thing next to impossible.

"*Will* you move your heinie?" I asked irritably as we went wobbling down Maple Tree Lane. "I can't see what's coming."

"Nothing's coming," said Alfred in tremulous tones, with white knuckles clutching the handlebars.

"I'd prefer to be the judge of that," I said, so he attempted to lean to the right, giving me about three inches of vision.

We went on like this for a while until my arms and legs ached and I decided that I hated his very guts, wished I had never met him, and that he had the biggest bottom in the United States of America. It was then that I leapt off and made him pedal. Oddly enough, this worked out somewhat more satisfactorily. For one thing, I was a better balancer than he was, so he was able to see more than I had. Even so, by the time we got to the Gambini farm, his arms and legs were shaking with fatigue and he had taken to barking, "Lean over! Lean over!" at increasingly annoying intervals. I leapt off and there would have been unpleasant words had we not at that moment espied what espied we did. There were seven short brothers grouped around the roof of a gingerbready farmhouse. As we watched, they flipped off the top and hung by their toes from the gutters.

"We have come," said Alfred, "not a moment too soon."

Ten

AS SOON AS THE GAMBINIS saw us, they did a series of swings and flips, until they landed all together at our feet.

"Alfredo!" they cried in gladsome tones.

They picked him up and began tossing him among themselves. Alfred turned somersaults in the air, he flipped, he flopped, he flew to dizzying heights to land on top of someone's shoulders. He balanced upside down on the soles of someone's feet. It was spectacular, to say the least. When he finally came back to rest by me, I stared at him.

"Why, Alfred," I said at last. "What unexpected talents."

"Some people are born to gymnastics, some people

strive for gymnastics, and some people have gymnastics thrust upon them," he said.

"Alfredo, Alfredo, Mama Mona is in the kitchen making spaghetti. You and your friend come in and have some pasta with us," said one of the brothers. They had been introduced to me one by one, but they were all about the same height and build, with the same short dark hair, and I kept getting mixed up about which was which.

"I've come on business," said Alfred. "Sort of."

"All good business begins and ends with spaghetti," said another brother, and we were ushered into the house.

A long wooden table was set with thick plates. When Mama Mona saw us she swept Alfred up into her arms and hugged him to pieces. Then, for good measure, she did the same to me. I think she was afraid I was someone she knew but had forgotten. Then when Alfred introduced us and she realized she didn't know me, she did it again. It was strangely thrilling. After that, everyone bustled around to put more plates on the table, which Mama Mona filled with huge mounds of spaghetti, sauce, and bread. For the second time that Saturday morning I ate myself sick. I don't know where Alfred put it all. He is of that thin wiry construction that can suck up food like a vacuum cleaner.

"So," said Alfred after we had all eaten a first plateful and Mama Mona was happily going around tossing more spaghetti anywhere she could find a vacancy.

"What are you doing here in town? Technically out of town. On a farm."

"Ah, Alfredo," said one of the Gambini brothers. "It was your mother, that gem of gems, that jewel of jewels, that tall Madonna of the circus, who gave us the idea. First of all, she wrote the snake lady a letter saying how much she enjoyed living in this nice town. How now she's got a tree. Well, some of the circus people, they went around tapping their heads and calling her loco, saying, 'She's gotta tree? So what?' Then the snake lady decided that she wanted a tree, too. And maybe, you know, like, a bush. So Elmira moved in and right across the street from that kind mama of yours. Then the snake lady sends us a letter. She says, you Gambinis, I got a tree. I got a bush. And guess what, I got a membership in the library. Then Mama Mona took the letter with her everywhere she went and we noticed that she kissed it and held it to her bosom. Mama Mona, we said, what's the matter? And Mama Mona admitted she wanted a tree, she wanted a bush, she wanted maybe a little plot of land to grow some herbs, some basil, some oregano, some garlic, to make her own spaghetti sauce again. So we said, 'Okay, Mama Mona, you traveled for us all these years, now we're gonna cash in those chips. We're gonna buy you a farm.' "

"Hmm," said Alfred. "You guys going to be farmers?"

At this, the whole table erupted in laughter, and Mama Mona laughed the longest and the loudest.

"These fellas? Farmers?" She guffawed. She ran

around the table and picked up Alfred and hugged him again. I feared for him and that plateful of spaghetti in his stomach. I really did.

"We're no farmers," said one of the Gambinis. "We're getting jobs."

"What kind of jobs?" asked Alfred when he had caught his breath.

"Well, we don't exactly know, but we'll find jobs. This is America, land of opportunity. Probably we'll drive into the big town and get jobs with the auto plant. Then at night we can come home and help Mama Mona with her herb garden."

"Hmm," said Alfred.

The same thought had probably occurred to him that occurred to me. If they were driving in the other direction to the auto plant to get work and if they lived way out here on the farm, then Springfield would hardly see them and might not even know they exist. No need to risk their feelings, asking them not to be peculiar.

"Well," said Alfred, "how come you need this huge farm if all you're growing is a few herbs?"

"Mama Mona likes space," said one of the brothers, and then we all ate some gelato and called it a day.

Of course, we should have known better than to think that the Gambini brothers could keep a low profile even if they wanted. The mere fact that they were the third circus family to move to Springfield was enough to drive the town wild. The following week

Mama Mona joined our church and entered her name in the bake-off, which should have been just fine. After all, it was supposed to be for everyone and I had seen the Gambinis in church and it wasn't like they took flying leaps off the altar or anything. They sat nice and quiet like everyone else, but some people were bothered by the fact that they were *there*. Some people even turned to stare rudely at them during the service. I wished Reverend Dwindle would do what our teacher at school does when someone does that and yell, "Eyes forward, Jenson!" but he didn't. He just looked more and more worried and helpless, which, of course, was extremely effective.

Then one day Mom came home in a huff. She usually doesn't let me in on any good grownup gossip, but that day she was so upset that she just blurted it all out.

"Oh, Ivy," she said, sitting down with a thump. I could see that her hands were shaking. "Some of the women at the church want to ban all circus people from the bake-off."

"*What?*" I asked. Alfred and I had just handed in our entry form for the peanut-butter pound cake and I was darned if I was going to withdraw it.

"The problem is that the snake lady entered something called snake cake and everyone is afraid she is going to put snakes in her cake. I said that no one would do such a thing. And of course it's just an excuse to be mean to the circus people."

"I don't understand," I said. "They aren't *doing* anything. They aren't hurting anyone and they all have jobs in town now. They aren't even part of the circus anymore. The snake lady is running her snake kennel and the Gambinis have all gotten jobs at the auto plant. Alfred's father is the only one who still actually works for a circus."

"It's perfectly stinking," said my mother, getting up and pacing. "And I won't have it. They're talking about property values and those queer Gambinis."

"Why?" I asked.

"I don't know. Everyone is careful not to talk about it too much around me. I'm sure there's enough people whose hearts are in the right place who wouldn't dream of excluding the circus people from the bake-off, but the problem is, you never hear from them. We could take a vote and probably the excluders would lose, but how would Georgina and the others feel if it came to a vote?"

"How would Alfred feel?" I said.

"Exactly," said my mother worriedly and began pacing again.

I was worried about it, too, but I didn't know what to do. Then trouble started at school. The boys whose parents were nastiest about the snake lady had started to taunt Alfred in the school yard and I feared that at some point I was going to have to bloody someone's nose. As I didn't know how to go about doing this, I found it very stressful. That Saturday saw me pacing alongside my mother until Alfred came over with that morning's classifieds. I had promised to go to garage sales with him to help him find a bike. We took a hammer to my piggy bank. I had $12.87, which I thought would be enough. There were lots of garage sales, it being the first week of May and spring-cleaning time, but we could find only three far-flung bikes. We went to the garage sale nearest our house first. The bicycle was pink.

"I think not," said Alfred.

We went to the second garage sale. They wanted twenty bucks for the bike and didn't seem interested in bargaining. The third house had a fairly decent bike and they were willing to take $12.87 in lieu of the fifteen dollars they had hoped for. Our hearts floated on spring's fragrant breezes as Alfred mounted his new green bike. Then we heard a familiar voice and there was a Gambini. When he saw us, he trotted right over.

"So, Alfred! So, Ivy!" he said, shaking our hands warmly. How I loved these enthusiastic greetings. "So, you made a purchase. I made a purchase, too."

"Really?" said Alfred. "I got a bike."

"It's a beauty," said the Gambini, stroking it appreciatively. "You want to come see my little beauty?"

We all walked over and looked where the Gambini pointed. But we couldn't figure it out.

"Where?" I asked finally as he patted the side of the garage.

"Right here, the little sweetheart," he cooed, patting the garage again.

We peered inside. It was full of junk.

"What did you buy?" asked Alfred, looking in.

"Why," said the Gambini, "I bought the garage!"

Eleven

WELL, IT TURNED OUT the Gambinis had bought about seventeen garages. They kept buying them and having them moved into their back field. It was a little odd, but as my mother says everyone ought to have a hobby. Alfred and I went over to see the garages. It looked kind of neat—all those garages scattered in the field. They were all different colors, no two were alike, I could see the attraction. There was nothing in them, the Gambinis weren't buying seventeen cars or anything. They just liked garages.

"It's okay with me, so long as they don't come crowding in my herb garden," said Mama Mona. "They're nice-looking garages, too, don't you think?"

"Yes," said Alfred and I. I understood now that this was partially to blame for the new wave of anti-circus feeling, but I didn't really see the problem. In fact, if you've gone along looking at nothing but cornfields long enough, a garage field is a welcome relief.

Alfred and I, when we weren't perfecting our peanut-butter pound cake, biked off periodically to play in the garages. We each had our favorite. I was enchanted with a black one with white shutters. Alfred liked one that was spray-painted lime green and was covered in graffiti. I considered it loud and tacky, although I didn't say so to Alfred. He was sensitive about his taste.

The Gambinis didn't mind us popping over any time, and when they were there they practiced throwing us around from roof to roof, something my mother wouldn't have approved of, I am sure, but there is nothing like the thrill of flying through the air on a bright spring morning. And Mama Mona would always invite us in and, in her good openhearted way, try to stuff us to bursting with heavy tomato-rich foods. It reminded me of my father and the French toast. There is something about happy expansive people that makes them want to see how much it takes to explode your stomach.

I became quite fond of those garages even before the day they saved our lives. It was a Thursday afternoon. Thursday afternoons can be tough. You've about had it with the week but the week hasn't had it with you. During recess, some of the older boys had started twitting Alfred, calling him monkey boy and other not very clever names. Finally, one of them grabbed his Tshirt sleeve and he fell off-balance on the blacktop and scraped his knee. I discovered that you can become so angry that you lose all fear. I stepped forward and kicked the boy who had hurt Alfred, as hard as I could. Believe me, this surprised me more than anyone, and there were a lot of sudden gasps on that blacktop. A monitor appeared at that moment and the boy I had kicked said, "After school, Ivy." When I had calmed down and regained my fear, I began to worry about after school.

"What am I going to do?" I kept writing on notes and passing them to Alfred about every ten minutes.

"I don't know," he kept writing back.

For someone who had had his rear end saved, he wasn't being very helpful.

When he got my ninth note he wrote, "Listen, as soon as the bell rings, we'll hop on our bikes and go to hide in the garages. They'll never find us there."

"What about tomorrow?" I wrote.

"We'll figure that out later," he wrote back.

"When later?" I asked.

"We may not even be alive later," he wrote back.

I could see his point. When it was time to get lined up at the door, Alfred and I managed to be first in line. As soon as the bell rang, we were on our bikes and out of there. Unfortunately, this had been anticipated by the goons of the playground, who had bigger bikes, and they were soon in hot pursuit.

I have never before, never since, and with any luck will never again pedal as I pedaled that day. We tried going up streets and down, cutting across yards, sneaking down alleys, but the goons remained behind us. When at last we reached the Gambinis' yard, we threw our bikes into the first garage we saw and ran through the fields. We chose a garage and flew into it, peeking out to see what the goons were up to. They were methodically going from garage to garage in search of us. My stomach was sick. Oh, to be left murdered and abandoned in one of these garages. There was nothing to do but wait.

"Goodbye, faithful friend," I whispered to Alfred.

"They wouldn't dare do anything really bad," said Alfred, but he didn't sound very hopeful.

As we heard their voices growing louder, we clutched each other's arms tensely. Then we heard something extremely unexpected.

"This is so rad," said one of them.

"This is so totally cool," said another.

"That kid's got some rad friends."

I noticed that all three of them talked exactly the same.

"So this is what my father thinks sucks."

"He thinks this sucks?"

"Yeah, he says it trashes the countryside."

"But these are so cool."

"I don't think they trash the countryside. I think they're totally rad."

I was ready to come out of hiding if only to put an end to this boring dialogue. Then they walked in and saw us.

"Hey, there they are," said one.

"Yeah, you're just the guy we've been looking for," said another.

Alfred and I stood up. Alfred put up his dukes. It was very theatrical of him and made him look pretty foolish, but I guess his heart was in the right place.

"Chill out," said one of them. "Say, your circus friends own these garages?"

"Yes," said Alfred warily.

"Cool."

"Totally rad," said another.

"For heaven's sake, can we use another word?" I shouted.

"Not now, Ivy," said Alfred, trying to frown at me and grin weakly at the hoodlums at the same time.

"Well, *when* then, Alfred?" I asked. "Someone has to tell them. Have they never heard of dictionaries? Have they never picked up a book? How many times can you hear 'rad' in a conversation?"

"Ivy, it's not a question of that. It's a question of choosing *this* particular *moment* to criticize their language!"

"I'm very language-sensitive," I said.

"Shut up, Ivy."

"No, you shut up!"

"You first!"

"No, you first!"

"Jeez Louise, guys," said one of the goons. "I'm gonna come over and make you *both* shut up."

"I'd like to see you try," I said.

"I wouldn't," said Alfred.

"Yeah, well, I *would*," I said.

"Wouldn't."

"Would."

"Wouldn't."

"Would."

"Both of you shut up!" yelled one of the goons. "I gotta question."

At least he didn't call Alfred monkey boy. I decided this was a good sign.

"I got, like, a model-car collection," the goon continued. "Do you think, like, maybe your friends would mind if I brought it over and put it in one of the garages? That would be so cool. So, can you introduce me to these friends of yours?"

"Yeah, well, maybe," said Alfred, "if you can be polite."

"Hey, we're cool," said one.

"Well, you haven't been very cool up to now," I said. "Threatening our very lives and limbs."

"Hey, she kicks me in the shin and then, like, she says *I* haven't been cool," said the one I kicked.

"Well, you hurt Alfred," I said.

"He tripped," said the kicked goon.

"He tripped because you grabbed his sleeve and threw him off-balance," I said.

"Whatever," said the goon.

"So we want no more trouble from you in the future," I said primly.

"Yeah, yeah," said the goon. "So what do you think,

Alfred? Like, will you introduce us to these friends of yours?"

"Well . . ." said Alfred.

"Come on, like we're sorry, okay. And we won't, like, even beat you to a bloody pulp or anything."

I think it was this stroke of diplomacy that turned the tide, because Alfred agreed.

"You can come with us Saturday morning," he said.

"Barfin," said one.

"Can we just stay and look around? Like, you think they'd mind that?"

"I don't feel I am in a position to grant you that privilege," said Alfred in stuffy tones. "Saturday."

"Hey, that's cool," they said.

We all walked back to our bikes self-consciously. None of us were friends exactly, but I was happy not to be hanging dead and bleeding from the gutters. Things had to go up from there.

Twelve

IN A WAY, things went up. In a way, things went
down. I said this to Alfred as we settled in the graveyard a few days later.

He gave me a long look. "It was the best of times,
it was the worst of times," he replied.

"Hey, that's good," I said. "You should save that for
one of your books."

"That's Charles Dickens, you ignoramous," said Alfred but I could tell he said it affectionately.

Alfred is the only person I know who has read more
than I have, and if you consider that until he moved to
Springfield he didn't even have a public library, that's
pretty impressive.

"The strong man had trunks of leather-covered

books. Nicer than those plastic-covered books from the library," said Alfred.

"My dad says that soon all books are going to be on computer screens," I said.

"That will certainly signal the end to civilization," said Alfred moodily, sitting on a tombstone and eating an apple. I don't know how he can eat in a cemetery. It seems kind of gross somehow, but he says that I am too sensitive and a graveyard is just a big park, really.

"A big park for the dead," I said, shivering.

"A big park for the living, Ivy. The dead don't use parks." He threw away his apple core and started on a chocolate bar.

"How do you know?" I asked. I didn't know he had a chocolate bar with him. Eating apples in a graveyard is gross, but somehow chocolate can be consumed anywhere. "I don't suppose you could spare a bite of that chocolate bar?" I asked. "You know that Milky Ways are my favorite."

Alfred sighed and handed over the chocolate. I took a large bite and handed it back. Alfred is the only person I could ever share bites of a chocolate bar with.

"Jeez, you ate half of it. I hate it when you do that," said Alfred. "Why don't you ever bring your own chocolate bars anywhere? You always pretend that you aren't going to get hungry and then you end up eating half of mine."

"I only took one bite," I said.

"We have had this discussion before," said Alfred coldly.

"Well, anyhow, the goons at school have stopped picking on you," I said, trying to change the subject.

"They want me to introduce them to the snake lady now so they can see the snakes," said Alfred glumly.

"But that's a *good* thing, Alfred," I said. "They'll become friends with the Gambinis and Elmira and then their parents will see that these people are nice and everything will be hunky-dory."

"We'll see," said Alfred.

"Don't be so pessimistic," I said. "What are the Gambinis entering in the bake-off?"

"I don't know," said Alfred. "Let's bike over and find out."

"You know we are never going to get our books written if we don't crack down," I said. "I don't even have my characters lined up yet and you haven't done anything on yours since the last time we met at the cemetery. Admit it."

"I've got a certain amount done," said Alfred evasively.

I wished he wasn't so secretive about his writing.

"If you've got so much done, tell me what it's about," I said.

"I don't believe I want to discuss my writing with you anymore," said Alfred. "When we're both done, we can show each other our books."

This really made me mad. "Well," I said in a huff, "have you given any more thought to the idea that *you* might be fictional?"

"I just hate it when you start that," said Alfred. "If I were fictional, could I do this?" Alfred leapt off the tombstone in what was meant to be a daring flip, but he landed on one knee and scraped all the skin off it. There was some leaping around and screaming about whose fault it was and we had to walk our bikes home instead of riding to the Gambinis' because it hurt him too much to pedal.

The Lutes were meeting at our house this week, so instead of being greeted by number-ten tin cans, we were treated to the twanging of instruments in the hands of varying degrees of musicianship. My mom was the virtuoso of the group. Alfred's mother was still learning and did not seem to have a natural bent for it. Alfred had gone home to put Band-Aids on his knees and think sour thoughts about me, no doubt. I had come in the back way and was on the porch swing unbeknownst to the two women who came into the kitchen to sneak cookies.

"I hear that Alfred Halibut has those rotten older children *hypnotized,*" said one of them.

"Can he do that, too?" asked the other woman.

"So they say. And God knows what other tricks he picked up in the circus," hissed the first one.

"It's just as we've been saying, Marian, you let one into the community and you leave the door wide open. And what's it going to take to get that woman to get rid of those snakes? Are we going to have to have a fatality first?"

"The mayor should do something."

"John called and told him so, but you know he says there's nothing *official* he can do."

"Well, you know what that means," said the other woman, and they ate a few more cookies and chuckled unpleasantly.

I would have stayed to hear more, but I saw Alfred limping up the driveway and I didn't want him exposed to any of this. He was gloomy enough as it was. I had never expected, before I knew Alfred, to meet anyone as gloomy as myself, much less end up spending my days bucking up someone's flagging spirits. Well, I thought fairly, if everyone wanted me out of town I guess I might flag a bit, too. As much as I wasn't really a people person, I took it for granted that any town would leap around and shout hooray at the sight of *me*.

I ran outside and convinced Alfred to get back on his trusty steed and we rode over to the Gambinis' and got ourselves tossed off roofs for a while and played with the goons, who were busy building little garages for their model-car collections inside the big garages. Then we stopped and helped Mrs. Gambini weed her herb garden and went into the house for biscotti, which are thick dry cookies that are pretty good dipped in milk. We ate a dozen or so of those before Mrs. Gambini was satisfied. We asked her what she was making for the bake-off.

"Zabaglione. Here, you sit yourselves down and I'll make you some right now," she said, patting us affectionately on the back.

"What is it?" I asked.

"It's custard with wine. You'll love it," said Mrs. Gambini.

Custard with wine? I shuddered. "Reverend Dwindle doesn't like puddings," I said.

"Everybody likes zabaglione," said Mrs. Gambini firmly. "And hey, you know what, Alfred? Mrs. Harrison is moving to town, too. She bought a house not that far from you. How about that?"

"Mrs. Harrison?" I asked.

"Fortune-teller," said Alfred, putting his head down on the table.

Thirteen

ACTUALLY, MRS. HARRISON the fortune-teller had married Mr. Wydel the strong man. Now she was Mrs. Wydel and they had both moved to town, so it was a twofer. Alfred's mom naturally was excited when they immediately invited her over, and decided to bring them a plate of homemade petits fours. Mrs. Halibut, try as she might, just never could get the hang of Midwestern cookery.

I wanted to go with them because I knew that with every arriving circus member the plot thickened. I was getting no writing done these days anyway because instead of coming home from school and heading up to my room to write and brood (not an unpleasant pastime, mind you), I was making the rounds with Alfred. First I had to rehash the day with him. Then we visited Elmira when she was home, and checked out her snakes and her garden; then up to see the Gambinis. I was even of nodding acquaintance with the goons, who were named Clarence, Leroy, and Al. We would never be bosom buddies, having such opposing views as we did on professional wrestling, but a quick howdeyado never hurt anyone. I was even taking a shot at improving their vocabulary.

"Rad," they would say.

"How very amusing," I would suggest as a possible alternative. Alfred said I sounded prissy and affected.

On the way to the Wydels', Mrs. Halibut strode manfully ahead of us. She found it impossible to slow herself to my or Alfred's pace, which was just as well, as it gave me a chance to quiz Alfred about the Wydels.

I especially wanted to meet Mrs. Wydel because I wanted her to read my fortune and tell me how all this tension in town was going to turn out and also whether we were barking up the wrong culinary tree with our peanut-butter pound cake.

"I don't see how anyone can possibly have any objection to the Wydels," said Alfred worriedly. "They don't go around jumping off roofs, they don't keep snakes, they're just a couple of old retired people."

"Were they dating when you knew them in the circus?" I asked. "Was true romance spouting from every pore?"

"I dunno," said Alfred.

Mrs. Halibut turned in at a pretty little cottage and knocked at the door. An immense man and a teeny woman answered it. They raced down the steps and hugged Alfred and Mrs. Halibut. Then Mrs. Halibut introduced me. Their manners, like most of the circus people's, seemed from an earlier, more formal era, so that when I was introduced to them I felt like an honored guest and not just another kid. I wondered if this was because, as Alfred had told me, a lot of them stayed in the circus generation after generation and didn't mix much with the outside world. Or maybe they were happy people, being able to do something they loved, and happy people made for better manners.

They ushered us inside to a book-lined house. Beautiful leather-bound volumes were everywhere. I wanted to grab one and find myself a hammock that very minute.

"I suppose you wonder why we invited you today," said Mrs. Wydel with twinkling eyes as she passed out teacups. Somehow it was hard to imagine her sitting in a tent covered in exotic jewelry, peering into palm after sweaty palm. She looked more like she should be at the Kmart on seniors day, scooping up the bargains.

"Why, Katie dear," said Mrs. Halibut. "Of course I wanted to see you as soon as you were settled."

"Well, I don't know about that," said Mrs. Wydel. "After all, you've been rather deluged by circus settlers lately. Started a regular stampede you have, and I bet it's as bad as having constant houseguests."

"Why, no trouble at all," said Mrs. Halibut, which goes to show you how clued out *she* was.

"Hmm," said Mrs. Wydel skeptically. "At any rate,

we have a surprise for you. We just got here today and someone hitched a ride with us."

"Well, my goodness, who is it?" asked Mrs. Halibut.

As we were all wondering which of their circus buddies had come, a man sprang out from behind a door very dramatically. Mrs. Halibut screamed and leapt up. Alfred started in his chair and jumped up, too, his hair pushed right off his face.

"*Reginald!*" screamed Mrs. Halibut.

"*Dad!*" screamed Alfred.

I certainly felt out of place. Mrs. Wydel came over and sat next to me and gave my hand a little squeeze.

"Don't you just love family reunions?" she whispered.

Alfred, Mrs. Halibut, and Mr. Halibut all started talking to each other swiftly, trying to catch up on news and speaking in the way that only families or close friends can.

"You mean you."

"Last night."

"Never told us that."

"But we were going to."

"Hailey's goldfish."

"Right fourteen blenkinsops."

"Frightwig."

And things of that nature. I am naturally nosey, but even if I had wanted to, there was no point trying to make any sense out of that conversation. You had to share the history. So I rose and excused myself, saying that I guessed I was superfluid.

"Superfluous," said Alfred.

Anyhow, he didn't deny it, so I smiled at all and sundry and backed out the door. Mrs. Wydel followed me. I could tell she was one of those people who is not only kindly but terrifically in tune with what everyone is feeling as well.

"You mustn't mind, dearie," she said as she walked down to the gate with me. "They haven't seen each other for a long time and they're none of them thinking straight. They'll go out and catch up and Alfred will probably fall over himself getting to you to tell you about it tomorrow."

"Can you really read the future?" I asked.

"Not really, dear," she said. "But what did you want to know?"

"About the bake-off—so much seems to be riding on it . . ."

"Oh, everything will work out, dearie. Don't go fretting about it."

She was a nice woman even if she couldn't read the future.

"What kind of a bake-off is it?" she asked.

So of course I told her about it and she promised to make some of her fortune cookies. I hoped no one on the casserole committee would think it unsanitary— all those little pieces of paper baked into cookies. I smiled, waved goodby, and headed on home.

My dad was lying on the couch reading the paper. My mom was making dinner.

"Is this my beloved bedraggled daughter?" he

shouted when I came in. "Are we actually seeing her before 6 P.M.? Has Alfred expired, my dear?" he asked, clutching me to his paternal bosom.

"Oh, Dad," I said. "What's for dinner?"

"Take a deep sniff," he said. I did.

"Corned beef," I said. "And cabbage."

"Have you ever smelled anything lovelier? Ah, Marie Antoinette is a diamond in the rough," he said, sighing, and went back to his paper. He always thinks that is a compliment and it drives my mother crazy. I think he means a jewel among women or something, but no matter how many times we point this out he always forgets and calls her a diamond in the rough.

I went in to see my mom. "Guess what?" I said, sticking my finger into the tapioca she was making for dessert. "The fortune-teller and the strong man have moved into town."

"Oh no," said my mother and stopped stirring. Stirring is crucial to tapioca, so that gives you some idea how upset she was.

"You know what I mean," she continued, hastily picking up the spoon again. "Things are getting so heated. They've started a petition to keep the circus people out of the bake-off. When Reverend Dwindle killed that, the same group wanted to make the snake lady hand in her recipe for snake cake."

"They can't do that," I said. "The recipes are secret. That's the point."

"Well, of course, but you know what they think she's putting in it, don't you?"

"Snakes, of course," I said.

"Right. As if someone *would* put snakes in a cake. How ridiculous! Besides, with mobs like this, they are simply trying to find subtle ways to make the circus people feel unwelcome."

"That's not very church-like of them, is it?" I asked.

"No, but unfortunately, dear, one of the things you learn when you get older is that churches aren't necessarily havens for good people. They are for everyone."

"Including circus people," I said.

"Well, we must make that point. But we must make it, Ivy, and this is important, we must make it without causing a big stir that will make the circus people uncomfortable."

"Mrs. Halibut doesn't even realize there's trouble," I said.

"Thank heavens for small favors," said my mother.

"But Alfred does and he's worried. It's not even the kids anymore. They've pretty much accepted him. But Alfred knows about these church people not wanting his family to stay in town. Pretty soon he'll be so unhappy he'll want to move. That would be awful."

"I'm glad you have a little friend," said my mother.

Little friend, indeed. There was a marked contrast between the courtesy and respect with which I was treated among my circus friends and my parents' persistent belief that eleven years old was little.

The next day, as Alfred and I walked home from school together, he seemed happy. It hadn't occurred to me that he had missed his dad so much. After all, he had *me*, didn't he?

"So, what do you want to do?" I asked. "Go to the cemetery and work on our books? Go to the Gambinis'? Feed one of Elmira's snakes? See how the Wydels are doing? What?"

"Well," said Alfred, shyly ducking his head, "I just sort of wanted to go home and see my dad."

"Oh, of course," I said, embarrassed. Then I felt guilty because one part of me hoped Mr. Halibut would have to leave town again soon. What was I supposed to do all afternoon without Alfred?

"We were going to toss a baseball around together in the backyard," he said.

"Oh, fine," I said, waiting for that old baseball invitation to come, but it didn't. So I went home, trying to look pathetic, but Alfred was having none of it. I went up to my room, took out my binoculars, and watched them boldly from the window, hoping Alfred would look up and see my haunting face. I knew for sure he knew he was being watched, but he didn't seem to care. Back and forth that baseball went.

Finally my mom came upstairs and pulled me away from the window. "For heaven's sakes, Ivy," she said. "What if the Halibuts see you? What are they going to think?"

"You didn't mind me doing this when I was sick," I said.

"Yes, but that was before we knew them," she said and pulled down the blind.

After that, I sulked and tried to write my book, but it was no go. My protaganist was a boy, and gosh, no matter what innocent thing he tried to do—go to school, eat dinner, go shopping—he was always eaten by a bear. So I sighed and went down to talk high finance with my dad. It made him happy and it provided me with some sound investment advice. I tried to remind myself that at one time in my life this would have been a full day.

This father father father business was no doubt a mark of character on Alfred's part, but he'd better snap out of it. The bake-off was soon.

Fourteen

THE REST OF THE WEEK was pretty much a carbon copy of that first day. Alfred played baseball with his father. He played basketball with his father. He played soccer with his father. It was like he was trying to get a whole year's worth of sports into one week.

"The bake-off is soon," I said to Alfred. "We ought really to figure out what we are going to do."

"I thought we were going to make a peanut-butter pound cake," said Alfred.

"Yes, but you can't just mix up a cake. You have to test it. To figure out some kind of gimmick for it. You want to win this thing, don't you?" He seemed less interested in the bake-off since becoming a sports fiend.

"As opposed to losing, sure," said Alfred. But I didn't think he took my point.

"Are we running a decathlon after school today?" I asked.

"My dad and I are playing lacrosse," said Alfred.

"Oh, *come on!*" I yelled. "Nobody plays lacrosse."

"Do you want to meet my dad?" asked Alfred.

"I've met him," said I.

"Do you want to play lacrosse with us?" asked Alfred.

"If I'm not intruding," I said in a lofty tone.

And so it was that I found myself in their big backyard trying to catch a ball in a basket. After a while we began to get really sweaty. Alfred and his father and I were about evenly matched. I suspected that up until that day they had never played lacrosse either.

Mr. Halibut wasn't very chatty, just shouting "Olé" now and again when he caught the ball. In truth, we none of us had much breath for chitchat, so busy were we running and sliding in the mud. At last, panting and sweaty, we decided to call it quits and sat down on the ground to get our breath.

"Mrs. Halibut and I would like to extend an invitation to you and your family to come for brunch tomorrow morning," said Mr. Halibut.

"Well, sure, I'd like to," I said. "But I'll have to ask my mom."

"I apologize for the lateness of the invitation," said Mr. Halibut. "But I only just now thought of it."

"Oh, no problem. We're rarely booked for Saturday mornings," I said.

"Perhaps we should ask your mother and inform Mrs. Halibut right now," said Mr. Halibut, rising.

So we went into the Halibuts' house, where the Lutes for Lent were rehearsing. When we came in, covered with mud, the ladies stopped playing and looked at us rather coldly.

"Dear ladies, keep luting," said Mr. Halibut. "I merely need to borrow my wife for a moment."

"Certainly, Mr. Halibut," said one of the ladies.

As Mrs. Halibut made her way toward the door, another woman spoke up, "Mr. Halibut, may I ask you a question?"

"Yes, indeed," said Mr. Halibut.

"Might we ask who to expect to move into town next? The ringmaster? Tightrope walker? Have you clowns in your circus?" She smiled at him.

Although it appeared on the surface to be a perfectly innocent question, several of the women smirked. Mr. Halibut looked around the room, slowly taking in everyone's expression and sorting things out.

"Well, of course, I don't work for the same circus, so I am not in touch in the way you seem to think," he began. "But I'm happy to think that whoever does leave our old circus to join us in town will be welcomed as warmly as we were."

Now, was that a speech or was that a speech? I felt like shouting bravo. Mr. Halibut went into the kitchen with Mrs. Halibut and arranged the brunch invitation. Then Lutes for Lent broke up and Mr. Halibut invited my mom for brunch. She said we'd be delighted and we went home. My mother and I didn't mention the incident between Mr. Halibut and the smirkers. What was the point?

The next morning at brunch, all seemed fine. The grownups sipped orange juice and champagne. Alfred and I had Hawaiian Punch. Then we sat around the big yellow table in the big orange room and talked cheerfully as if nothing had happened the day before.

I was relaxing and breaking off another cinnamon roll to stuff down my gullet when my mother said, "How do you like it here so far, Mr. Halibut?"

"It seems like a lovely town. It's such a pity that we have to leave." He smiled, but his voice was grim.

"*What?*" I screamed, spewing forth cinnamon-roll crumbs like April rain.

"Yes. You see I have found a town farther ahead, up by Illinois, that is even nicer, hard as that is to believe, and we will be putting our house on the market shortly."

I looked at Alfred, but he mouthed "Later" to me. As soon as it was politely possible, I pulled Alfred outside and let the grownups chat away in the living room.

"Alfred, what is this all about?" I practically shouted.

"Well, yesterday after everyone had left, my dad had conniptions. He said he could tell we weren't wanted in town. He had seen this kind of thing before and he wouldn't leave his wife and son in a hostile environment while he went off for weeks at a time. He had actually been planning on quitting his job as a publicist and getting a job in town, but he could see now that this would hardly be politic, considering how people here already hate us."

"People don't hate you. You can't move," I said.

"It's not up to me, Ivy," said Alfred, flicking his hair out of his face to show me how angry his eyes were. "If my dad says we have to move, there's nothing I can do."

"There must be something we can do," I said. "He can't take you away. And what about the other circus people in town? And what if the same thing happens in your new town? No, you must stay and fight."

Alfred shrugged.

"I'm going to do something," I declared stoutly.

"Like what?" asked Alfred.

"Just wait," I said.

The first thing I did was to start a reverse whispering campaign. I figured if people could go around and whisper unpleasant things about the circus people, I could go around and whisper pleasant things. As you may well imagine, this involved talking to quite a lot of people, which, as we all know, is not my strong suit. I tackled the goons first.

"Did you know," I said to them as they played in one of the Gambini garages, "that Alfred may have to move out of town because there has been so much talk about the circus people?"

"What a shame," said one of the goons.

"Too too dreadful," said Clarence.

"I shall miss him immensely," said Al.

"That's all very well," I said, wondering if I had

taken their speech too far in the opposite direction,
"but what are we going to do? What is our personal re-
sponsibility in the matter? Perhaps we should talk to
our parents about making them feel more welcome."

"I fear my father is rather partial to his own ideas.
He would be a forbidding wall up against which one
would not want to come," said Leroy.

"What a delightful metaphor," said Al.

"Charming," said Clarence.

"Well, here's another wall for you," I said. "If he
goes, the Gambinis might go, and if the Gambinis go,
their garages go!" I stormed out.

The next thing I did was to circulate during recess
and try to rally some support from the other kids. A
lot of them didn't even know there *were* circus people
in town. Some of them didn't care and some of them
didn't grasp the problem, but the good eggs promised
to help out if they could in some way.

Finally, I went to speak to Mr. Halibut. I did all
these things behind Alfred's back. He gets so worried
about stuff. The last thing I needed was him dithering
about gumming up the works.

I asked Mr. Halibut to meet me at the drugstore
soda fountain (because a man drinking a strawberry
soda is a man ready to listen to reason).

"Mr. Halibut," I said, taking a long slurp of my soda
and getting a strawberry caught at the end of the
straw, necessitating several rude noises before I could
free it, "I will get right down to why I have asked for
this meeting."

"I know why you have asked for this meeting, Ivy," said Mr. Halibut. "An old ad and publicity man like myself always has one ear to the ground. You don't want us to move and you are going to try to prove how much everyone wants us to stay."

Well, this certainly took the wind out my sails. It was exactly what I had planned to say, only I had planned to build to it gently.

I sucked meditatively on the pink foam for a minute before saying, "Well . . . yeah."

"Admirable, admirable, and don't think I won't remember the good along with the bad when we have gone."

This did not sound promising.

"But, you see, Mrs. Halibut has finally begun to suspect that the very ladies she cavorts with are not all wholeheartedly her friends. Mrs. Halibut is a rare and delicate flower, one of humanity's orchids, and we mustn't let her feelings get bruised. She wilts. How she wilts."

I tried to imagine large and footful Mrs. Halibut as a delicate flower. It is not the metaphor I would have choosen.

"What about Alfred?" I asked. "This is his *home* now. What about *his* feelings?"

"Naturally, I will take all feelings into consideration, even yours, Ivy dear. But I fear we have made a mistake in coming here. We came here innocently as ourselves. Our friends in the circus made no attempt to hide their past. I can see from now on we shall have to be more circumspect in order to have a peaceful existence."

"No, no, no, that's all wrong," I said and drained the last dregs of my soda. "Didn't you ever hear that song 'I'm So Glad to be Me'?"

"Well, you can't live your life by song titles, Ivy," said Mr. Halibut.

"I am me," I began to sing. Whenever I find myself singing in public, I know I am in trouble.

"Would you care for another soda, or are you through?" asked Mr. Halibut politely.

"Not you or he," I sang. "I'd like another, and hey, how about chocolate this time?"

"Well, all right, maybe one more," said Mr. Halibut, who looked as if the second-soda habit had been long ago established.

"Such a wonderful me, I wish I were three," I sang on.

"Please, Ivy," said Mr. Halibut, beginning to get sweaty around the collar. "I assure you I know all the lyrics."

"Okay, make a deal with me," I said, buying time. "Just come to the bake-off. If you come to the bake-off and you really think there is hostility to circus people, then move. By all means, move. But if you come and we have town people and circus people together and everyone gets along, then you must admit that you have been a tad oversensitive. Okay?"

Mr. Halibut took a sip of his new soda. "How are we going to gauge this, uh, hostility?" he asked.

Ah, I thought gleefully, first get them into the tent. But now that he was in the tent I didn't know what to do with him. Then I had a sudden inspiration. "If someone from the circus wins the bake-off, you can't say the town is against you. Especially if there is no big protest. There's a lot of hot competition to win this thing, you know, and there are always feuding factions, and if people are going to make a fuss about the circus people, it will come to a head at the bake-off, I assure you."

I didn't actually know this.

Mr. Halibut slowly sipped his soda. He looked around the drugstore walls.

"I like an old-fashioned drugstore," he said. "Most towns don't have them anymore, you know. Everything is malls now. I'd like to live someplace where I could get a soda on a Saturday morning with my boy."

"Well, then, are we on?" I asked, trying my best to look like a cocker spaniel. It is a look that works wonders with my own father, but a look that spells soft fuzzy animal in need of petting to one's parents may as easily spell mangy ratface to the general public.

"All right, I'll wait for the bake-off before passing judgment," said Mr. Halibut.

"That's not good enough!" I said, thinking of all the work I was going to have to do to ensure a happy pro-Halibut feeling at the bake-off. "I want this to be definitive. I want a definite yes or no at that bake-off. I want the bake-off to decide things one way or another. I think that's only fair."

Mr. Halibut stopped drinking. "What does Alfred

do when you flap around like this?" he asked, but he was smiling.

"Alfred," I said truthfully, "is one of those quiet types with a will of iron. I may flap around and make a lot of noise, but Alfred just moves things quietly the way he wants them to go."

"Well, I can't promise anything except that I will be as fair as I can be," said Mr. Halibut.

He finished his soda, sighed, and paid for us. I thought this was very nice of him, since I had been the one to call the meeting.

"We'd better head on home now for dinner," he said.

I wondered how Mr. Halibut was going to fit dinner in on top of those two sodas. I, myself, belched discreetly all the way home.

Fifteen

ALFRED WAS BITING his nails. I had told him on several occasions to stop this and even called him alligator fingers a couple of times to goad him into quitting, but it had no effect.

"You know," I said to him, "it would be easier if you *were* fictional. I could write you as a less worried sort. Everything is going to be fine. I am arranging everything according to plan." In a way, this was true; I *was* arranging everything according to plan, and as I didn't have a plan, I hadn't made any arrangements.

"Okay, tell me," said Alfred, heaving himself up on a tombstone, for we were back in our old haunt, the cemetery. This time I had brought chocolate bars for both of us.

"I think you're better off not knowing," I said.

"You don't have a plan, do you?" asked Alfred.

"What makes you say that?" I asked, hedging.

"Because it would be like you," said Alfred. "You're all full of emotions and short on method. That's why you get nothing done. That's why you haven't gotten beyond chapter 1 in your book."

"I didn't get beyond chapter 4 because my characters moved in next door and there's something not nice about writing about your neighbors."

"Nonsense," said Alfred. "Done all the time. And we're really very little like the people that you wrote about. It was just an excuse to stop writing."

"It was not!" I said, stung.

We ate our chocolate bars in sullen silence.

"Listen, Ivy," said Alfred after a while in kinder, gentler tones. "I want to stay in town, too. There's no point in you going off and trying to save me or whatever you have in mind. I know you are just trying to be discreet, but let's face it. I know what's going on, and if you don't mind, I'd rather help save myself, because there's some chance then that we might actually come up with a plan that works."

I screwed up my forehead. It was quite a speech. Was it a compliment or an insult? I thought rather on the whole that I had been affectionately insulted. But I decided to give up and let Alfred help me, because while I was sure that I *could* come up with a perfectly good plan all by myself, it wouldn't be as much fun to implement it alone.

"Okay, Alfred old boy," I said, putting my wrapper

back into my pocket and pacing around on Myrtle Mavisbine's head. "I talked to your dad and he has agreed
that if there is no sign of hostility at the bake-off and
if someone from the circus wins the bake-off and there
isn't a fuss, then you can stay in town, no hard feelings,
as it were. Maybe. At least I think that's what he
agreed to."

"Uh-hmmm," said Alfred. He got the sleepy look he
gets when his great brain is at work. He pulled his
knees into his chest. Then he glanced up, met my eyes
with his own piercing ones, and said, "It's quite easy,
actually."

"Oh, yeah?" I said.

"Yes, we will go to Reverend Dwindle and ask him
to fix the contest."

"What do you mean, fix it?" I asked.

"We will ask him to choose a circus person in ad-
vance to award the prize to. We shall simply explain
to him that it's for the good of the community, and we
shall ask that the anti-circus people be somehow shut
out from the event."

We immediately rode our bikes over to the church,
where, luckily, Reverend Dwindle was hard at work on
Sunday's sermon. It took no time at all to explain to
him the reason why we had come. He listened carefully
and then sighed, took his glasses off, pinched the
bridge of his nose, and looked over our heads. Alfred
and I both turned around automatically to see if there
were any angels floating by, but if there were, they
were only for the eyes of Reverend Dwindle.

"I am well aware of the tensions in the church," he said and sighed again.

"Well," I piped up, "don't you see that this would fix things? We have to embrace these circus people and show the anti-circus people that they are in the wrong."

"I agree with you," said Reverend Dwindle. "But there are many tensions, among many factions, not just the circus one. And they all want me to fix the bake-off."

"*What?*" I said. I had no idea that Alfred's solution was so popular.

"In fact, you are the seventh group, if two people can be called a group, that has come in today."

"Who else?" I asked.

"Never mind," said Reverend Dwindle. "What no one seems to take into account is the basic dishonesty of fixing a contest."

"It's just a means to an end," said Alfred.

"Well," said Reverend Dwindle, rubbing his eyes again. "In a sense there is no end, so the means we use are the only thing of any importance."

"I guess you don't plan to fix it, then," I said hastily, because I didn't want to get into a long philosophical discussion when time was of the essence. "What about banning the anti-circus people from the bake-off until they can behave themselves?"

Reverend Dwindle looked pained. "I'm sure everyone can think of someone or someones they would like banned from every church event. You will have to learn to get along with the anti-circus people just as much as they will have to learn to get along with you. This is what I am trying to impress on everyone, the importance of getting along."

It was at this point that Alfred and I decided we must indeed be getting along.

"Okay, no hard feelings, see you Saturday," I said and stood up.

The Reverend Dwindle gave us a weary wave. His parishioners are going to give him a nervous breakdown someday.

"Now what?" I asked Alfred as we pedaled home.

"Well, obviously the next thing to do is make sure that one of the circus people makes something extraordinary. Considering how little time we have left until the bake-off, I don't think this is too likely, do you, Ivy? I think we can immediately, for instance, write off snake cake and zabaglione as big winners."

"Maybe he'll have an unexpected passion for peanut-butter pound cake," I said glumly.

When we got home, we just had time to get changed and washed. We were invited to the Gambinis' for dinner that night. Mrs. Gambini was in one of those spaghetti moods of hers. By the time we got there, quite a few people from town were sitting around drinking Chianti on the porch, in the kitchen, and in the living room. Several kids had climbed on the garage roofs and were sloshing lemonade about. I had no idea the Gambinis had made so many friends already. Even the goons were there, without their parents, of course, who were part of the anti-circus crowd.

Mrs. Gambini, warm, gay, and dressed all in black as usual, was heaving loaves of hot bread out of the oven and flinging spaghetti in all directions, while those indistinguishable Gambini brothers raced about with bottles, laughing and slapping people on the back and pouring drinks.

"You see?" I said to Alfred. "Does this look like a town that doesn't like circus people?"

Mrs. Gambini shoved loaded plates in our hands and Alfred and I took them to a roof, where we sat among the goons.

"What a delightful evening," said Leroy.

"With such a mild spring, summer should be a balmy enchantment," said Clarence.

" 'April comes like an idiot, babbling and strewing flowers,' " said Al.

"Edna St. Vincent Millay?" said Leroy.

"Of course," said Al.

How like a female Frankenstein I felt.

"Let's get out of here," I whispered to Alfred and we shinnied down off the roof and settled ourselves on the porch railing of the house. By then everyone had eaten all they could and the adults began to weary, so we all settled comfortably while the Gambini brothers did some of their tricks in front of a sun setting large and orange on the field horizon.

Afterwards, I let myself be dragged sleepily to the car by my father, who was smiling and smoking a pipe with the deeply contented look he wears most of the time. I waved to Alfred, who didn't see me because his hair was totally over his eyes. Maybe he was sleeping. Maybe he was thinking. I hoped if he was thinking, he was thinking hard.

That night I lay in bed and worried and worried and worried. I thought how my life had been before Alfred, how I never did anything but come home and play in my room. How I never sat around on roofs eating spaghetti, just enjoying what everyone else was enjoying. I got up, took a flashlight, and tried to flash it at his window. I still hadn't gotten his attention when my mother came into my room.

"I thought I heard you prowling about," she said. "What's the matter?"

"I'm worried about the bake-off," I said. "I'm worried that the Halibuts will move out of town. I can't think of a plan to save them."

A tear or two dimmed my eyes. This embarrassed both my mother and me and we looked away from each other.

"Don't take it too hard," said my mother. "You can't always fix everything. Even if you had a plan, it might not work. Maybe things will work out on their own. A lot of people *do* like the circus people."

"I'm worried about the ones who *don't*," I said.

"Go to bed, Ivy," said my mother. "Que sera sera." She kissed me and went back to bed.

I could see what Mr. Halibut meant about not living your life by song titles.

Sixteen

FRIDAY NIGHT. What can you say about the Friday night before the Saturday bake-off? It came. It came as Friday nights do once a week whether you want them to or not. It came even though I wasn't ready for it.

Alfred and I were in the kitchen making the peanut-butter pound cake for the bake-off. My mother had already made her lute lovelies. These were little meringues filled with strawberries and gunk. They looked quite nice, although what they had to do with lutes was anyone's guess. My father said they were the best lute lovelies he had ever tasted.

"This pound cake doesn't *smell* that great," said Alfred as we sat at our kitchen table waiting for it to finish baking, and playing gin rummy.

"It smells the way it always smells," I said, for we had had two trial runs.

"No, it doesn't," said Alfred. "It smells more peanut-buttery or something."

"You're just nervous," I said. "Gin."

"We're not going to win the prize," said Alfred.

"I don't care about that anymore," I said. "The only thing that matters is that *someone* from the circus wins."

My mother came in. "Kids, kids," she said, bustling around and putting on makeup while looking into the side of the toaster. "The casserole ladies are going to be here very soon. Is that cake almost done?"

"Ten more minutes," I said, looking at the clock.

"Well, okay," she said. "Then hurry and clean up after yourselves."

At last the peanut-butter pound cake came out. It looked okay. We put it on a wire rack to cool and then moved our gin game to the back porch off the kitchen. The lilacs were in bloom and the smell wafting in on the twilight air made me feel better. How could anything nasty happen at such a beautiful time of year?

The usual suspects filed in and chatted amiably, drinking the coffee my mother had made and eating quite a few of her chocolate-chip cookies. Alfred and I could see into the kitchen easily from the window behind the porch swing, where we rocked and discarded.

"Well, I say we ask her. Before it's too late. We can't put Reverend Dwindle at risk like that," said one of the women in a louder voice.

"What are you talking about?" asked my mother, coming over to the offending voice.

"Lydia dear, I know that Elmira is a friend of yours, but we are going to demand to know what her secret baking ingredient is. We all know that her entry is entitled snake cake. Can there be any doubt?"

"Oh, you wouldn't," said my mother worriedly. "But it wouldn't be fair. No one else is being asked for their list of ingredients. Why, she would think that you thought . . ."

"But that's precisely what we *do* think," said one of the anti-circus people. "And we have every intention of asking. We can't let Reverend Dwindle poison himself, now, can we?"

Alfred's mother wasn't at the casserole meeting that night. She and Mr. Halibut were going to dinner and the movies together, as he had to go back to the circus in a couple of days. So, fortunately, she was spared this conversation, but Alfred heard it and he looked grim.

There was the sound of more heated discussion, but at that moment we saw Elmira coming up the driveway. Everyone usually came in through the back door, as it entered on the kitchen. Elmira stopped to chat with us on the way.

"Evening all," she said. "I joined something else today." She looked quite pretty in a grotesque way, smiling happily through her crooked teeth.

"How nice," I said in a too loud voice, trying to warn those inside of her approach.

"I joined the automobile association. And do you know what? As part of your membership they will fill out a whole vacation package for you. You give them your ultimate destination and they tell you everything you can see on that stretch of road. Isn't that wonderful? Do you know there are seven major tourist attractions between here and Chicago? And do you know that they didn't even care that I didn't own a car? They said if I didn't mind, they didn't mind. It was just marvelous. Do you want to see my membership card?"

Alfred and I admired it, and Elmira smiled broadly and went tripping in, a sheep to the slaughter.

Elmira's first clue should have been the silence with which she was greeted. Then my mother came rushing up and tried to get a great deal of action going at once. She started water boiling and cans opening and meat frying. But an uneasy silence lingered over all. Finally Mrs. May said, "WHY THE HECK IS EVERYONE SO QUIET? I KNOW I CAN'T ALWAYS HEAR *WHAT* PEOPLE ARE SAYING, BUT I CAN HEAR THEY ARE SAYING *SOMETHING.*"

Alfred and I gave up all pretense of playing cards and spied unashamedly on them through the window. One of the circus ladies put down her can and smiled kindly at Mrs. May, but it was a horrible smile.

"Well, we want to ask Elmira something, and I guess it's on our minds," said one of the ladies.

"I'D LIKE TO ASK HER SOMETHING MYSELF!" roared Mrs. May. "SINCE WHEN DO LADIES GO

AROUND GETTING THEMSELVES TATTOOED?
IT'S BAD ENOUGH FOR MEN, BUT WHY WOULD
YOU WANT TO RUIN YOUR SKIN WITH THOSE
THINGS?"

"Oh, my," said Elmira and blushed.

I was furious. Just because you're old doesn't mean you have the right to be rude. How would Mrs. May like it if someone commented on the fact that her slip usually fell unevenly six inches beneath her hem? And her myriad sweater-and-blouse layers weren't very attractive, either.

"Oh, my," said Elmira. "Well, it was the thing, you know, being the snake lady." The last came out whispered. I think it had just now occurred to her that maybe being the snake lady was a shameful thing to be.

"Well, *I* like tattoos. Distinguished. Thinking of getting one myself," said my mother. Good old Mom. "Right here," she said, pointing to one of her shoulder blades. "Small rose."

"WHAT'S THAT?" asked Mrs. May.

"Lydia is thinking of getting a tattoo! A small rose!" shouted one of the anti-circus ladies.

"WELL, YOU SHAMELESS HOYDEN," said Mrs. May. "IS IT CREAMED-CORN TIME?"

No one had cooked for several minutes and everyone momentarily picked up their various tasks silently again.

"NOW, WHY IS EVERYONE BEING SO QUIET?"

shouted Mrs. May. "WE SETTLED THE MATTER
OF THE TATOOS. DIDN'T WE SETTLE THE MAT-
TER OF THE TATTOOS?"

Mrs. Johnson put down her can and yelled, "Yes, of
course it's Elmira's business if she wants a tattoo.
That's personal and doesn't affect others, but there's
something that does affect others, and I fear we must
raise the subject, as it is on everyone's mind."

"Why, what is it?" asked Elmira, now thoroughly
whipped. I wanted to rush in and put my arms around
her and tell her that they were just a bunch of mean-
ies and to pay no attention to them, but sometimes
things move forward dreamlike as if everyone always
knew this was coming someday and I could see that
Mrs. Johnson, the nastiest anti-circus lady, had been
willing this meeting for a long time.

"We want to know what is in your snake cake. An
itemized list of ingredients," said Mrs. Johnson, smiling snake-like herself.

"Whatever for?" asked the snake lady. "Who wants
this list? I was told that all ingredients should be a secret, to keep people from copying recipes. Who has
changed the rules?"

"No one has changed the rules," said Mrs. Johnson,
now thoroughly enjoying herself. "All the rules are exactly the same. We are making an exception in your
case, my dear, as we are afraid you might be entering
something which we feel is unsafe for human con-
sumption."

"My snake cake?" asked Elmira in disbelief. "But,

but Lydia has eaten my snake cake. And the children. And the Halibuts. They'll tell you what a fine cake it is. Why should I have to say what's in it any more than you should say what's in your dessert?" All glow, all joy had disappeared from Elmira like air from a balloon. What was left of her sat at the kitchen table, alone, helpless, and humiliated.

"Because," said Mrs. Johnson, "we fear there may be something, shall we say untoward, going into your cake."

"SNAKES," said Mrs. Meyer, clearly having had enough of this dancing about.

The eviler of the women stared defiantly at the weeping Elmira, the less evil looked at their feet, the women who sided with my mother or fence-sat cleared their throats and said, Nonsense, ridiculous, and such, in low tones.

"This is outrageous!" said my mother. "And I won't have any more of it."

"Oh, indeed?" said Mrs. Johnson, raising her eyebrows as if to imply that given half a chance my mother would put snakes in her lute lovelies, too.

Elmira didn't say any more. She was crying quite loudly now and she stood up, slammed the porch door behind her, and dashed down the back steps.

"Well," said my mother, "talk about raining on someone's parade!" After that, she sputtered noiselessly, utterly at a loss for words.

"WHAT HAPPENED?" yelled Mrs. May.

"Oh, my. Who would have guessed a circus person

could be so sensitive? And it was really a perfectly harmless question. Pity she had to take it in that spirit," said Mrs. Johnson with satisfaction.

"I'm going over to Elmira's," said my mother, snatching up her sweater. "And I'm going to insist she put that snake cake in the bake-off and I'm going to tell her under no circumstance is she to give anyone a list of her ingredients and if I hear any more of this, why, you'll have *me* to answer to." And she stormed out.

"IS EVERYONE LEAVING?" asked Mrs. May. "AM I SUPPOSED TO HOLD THIS CREAMED CORN FOREVER?"

The ladies went back to making the casseroles and no one said another word.

Seventeen

THE NEXT MORNING was not a whole lot of fun.
My mother was taking everyone to the bake-off in our
van. She had convinced the snake lady to come with us,
although that wasn't such a feat. Elmira came out to
the van shrunken, beaten, and shamed. You could have
convinced her to do anything you liked, so deflated
was she. Her shoulders were hunched and she carried
a Tupperware cake container. I remembered sadly the
day she had come over to the house to tell us happily
about the two hundred dollars' worth of Tupperware
she had bought. It was a moment of arrival as far as
she was concerned. Now she had learned that sometimes, no matter how much Tupperware you buy, you
are unwanted.

But as dreadful as it was, seeing her like this, it was

worse to see Alfred. He had simply stopped speaking. He had totally retreated under his shock of black hair. His eyes, when I could see them, were like stones.

"Speak!" I said once in exasperation.

"That's not funny," he said.

"Come on, Alfred, it's not over," I said. "I brought our peanut-butter pound cake."

"It's over," said Alfred.

Alfred had protected his parents from the previous evening's unpleasantness, but they kept glancing at huddled Elmira and frowning.

My mother pulled up in front of the church and unloaded people and desserts with grim determination. She reminded me a bit of John Wayne in one of those old movies.

The church hall was decorated with the usual tacky bake-off decorations. They let the Sunday School classes do this. The Sunday School teachers, in between drilling the Ten Commandments into their student's heads, had enlisted everyone to cut out pictures of desserts from magazines and paste them on mobiles and poster board. I wouldn't exactly call it festive.

Long tables were set with white linen cloths on top of which were cards with the name of each dessert that was being entered. This year you had to open the card to find the name of the person submitting the dessert. Reverend Dwindle thought of that. Anyone could take a peek to see who had entered a dessert, but Reverend Dwindle would remain in blissful ignorance.

My mother found Alfred's and my entry card and

we put the peanut-butter pound cake there. Then my mom found her own lute-lovely card and the snake-cake card. Having accomplished that, she deposited the snake lady with my dad, who was to guard her. There is something about my dad's utter faith in the goodness of people that keeps them from doing anything nasty around him. Alfred and I trotted off behind my mother. She buttonholed Reverend Dwindle. He was eyeing the dessert tables and looking decidedly green.

"Reverend Dwindle," she said, grabbing his sleeve.

He kept looking at the dessert tables.

"Reverend Dwindle, what *is* the matter?" she snapped. I could tell that she was upset, because she never snaps and certainly not at a minister.

"Hmm? Sorry. Do you know it has just occurred to me that I am going to have to *taste* all that stuff?"

"You should have thought of that before you said you'd be judge," snapped my mother again.

"Well, yes, I suppose I should have, but really it never occurred to me before. You know maybe next year we should have a panel of judges."

"Maybe next year we should just skip the whole bake-off. It's more trouble than it's worth. Come into your office. I want to speak to you right now."

Was this my mother snapping and ordering a man of the cloth about?

We went silently down the hall to Reverend Dwindle's office. I think my mother had forgotten about me and Alfred.

"Now listen to me, Charlie," she said. I knew Reverend Dwindle's first name was Charles, but I had never heard anyone call him that, let alone Charlie.

"You're going to give that prize to the snake lady. I absolutely insist upon it."

Reverend Dwindle sighed and sat wearily down. I think if he had had less self-control he would have rolled his eyes. You could just hear him thinking, Here we go again.

"Lydia, we can't fix this thing. I don't know how many people have asked."

"You really do not understand," said my mother, and she explained the previous day's appalling incident.

Reverend Dwindle looked serious. He shook his head. "It's unfortunate that these things happen. I hope we all learn something and I hope we can persuade Elmira that she is indeed wanted, but I cannot fix the bake-off. It would be dishonest."

"Well, you're no help at all," barked my mother, standing up. "I can see I am going to have to take matters into my own hands."

"Now, Lydia, don't be hasty," said Reverend Dwindle.

"I'll be anything I want to be," said my mother, and she stormed back into the church hall.

We followed my mother as she paced about.

"By gosh, I know what I'm going to do," said my mother after ten minutes. She marched over to her dessert card, scratched out her name, and put the snake lady's name down.

"I don't get it," I said.

"Don't you see, Ivy?" said my mom. "The more desserts the snake lady's name is on, the better chance she has of winning."

She marched over to our peanut-butter pound cake and put Elmira's name on that, too. Naturally I would have agreed, but she could have at least asked. Then she went and whispered something to Mrs. Halibut, and Mrs. Halibut, smiling, crossed her own name out on her card. It was a good idea, but why stop there, I thought, and whispered this to Mom. Soon my mom, Mrs. Halibut, and I were busy mingling with the crowd, explaining things, staying carefully away from anti-circus folk. More and more people started heading to the dessert table to change the name on their cards to the snake lady's. Before long, the anti-circus people got wind of things and tried to make us stop. When they couldn't, they started heading to the table, scratching out the names on their cards, and putting down Mrs. Johnson. Reverend Dwindle was oblivious to the subterfuge and there was no reason why he shouldn't remain oblivious until it was time to reveal the winner. It would be either Mrs. Johnson or the snake lady.

Finally it was time for the judging to begin. We had done all we could do and we sat in chairs biting our nails along with Alfred. Alfred remained his stonelike self, Elmira sort of flapped loosely in the wind like a limp flag, also oblivious of the subterfuge. My father smiled benevolently on the proceedings. Mr. Halibut looked watchful. Mrs. Johnson smiled meanly. Everyone else had a hushed, expectant air. The suspense hung over us like smog.

Naturally, it took Reverend Dwindle a good long time to finish tasting. He waddled up one table and down the next, a prey to burping and unseemly skin color. It took him a long time to make his decision. You could have cut the atmosphere with a knife. At last he handed the winning card to Mrs. May. As the oldest citizen in the church, Mrs. May announced the winner each year. She tottered up to the microphone. You could always count on her announcing it loud and clear.

"THE WINNER IS ELMIRA DEGOOCHY," she read out.

A great cheer went up, and Elmira inflated again. It was miraculous. You could actually see the bloom going back into her cheeks. This time, tears of joy streamed down her face as she raced up to collect her prize. As she got to the microphone, someone in the audience yelled, "What did she win it for?"

"WHAT?" asked Mrs. May.

So Reverend Dwindle leaned over and repeated it in Mrs. May's ear.

"WHY, FOR HER DESSERT, OF COURSE!" yelled Mrs. May in the tone of one who has been asked an idiot question.

"What dessert?" came another voice.

"HUH?" asked Mrs. May, and Reverend Dwindle, who frankly looked ready to throw up, leaned over and talked in her ear again.

"OH," said Mrs. May, and turned the card over and read, "MINT CUPCAKES!"

Elmira, who had the microphone in her hand, stopped and said, "But I didn't make mint cupcakes. I made snake cake."

"Never mind, never mind," came several hurried shouts from the audience. "Hurry up and take the prize."

"DIDN'T *MAKE* MINT CUPCAKES?" said Mrs. May. "WELL, IT'S GOT YOUR NAME ON IT RIGHT HERE."

"FRAUD!" shouted someone from the audience.

And then someone threw a pie. They threw it at my mother. My father looked over and blinked. Mr. Halibut looked at me. Someone else, in sympathy with my mother perhaps or perhaps becaused it just looked like fun, threw a cake at the person who threw the pie. One of the leaders of the local Brownie troop picked up Mrs. Wydel's fortune cookies and began bouncing them off the other leader like squash balls. There was probably a story there. Mrs. Johnson, who was by then sporting chocolate custard with a certain aplomb, looked down to find a young child licking it off her. She gave him a look he would not soon forget. Brothers and sisters heaved cheesecakes to score off each other. I thought the desserts should have been used to settle larger issues myself. It became a dessert free-for-all and no one came out of that church that day without some whipped cream or strawberry glaze about the ears.

Mrs. May, who was watching everything and never did know what had been going on from the time the circus people started arriving, kept shouting, "WHAT THE HECK IS GOING ON?" at intervals. The Reverend Dwindle, who looked like he couldn't believe his eyes, kept shouting answers in her ear. Elmira looked as if she had no idea how to feel. She wasn't even sure what all this was about.

As more and more answers were shouted in her ear, Mrs. May looked crosser and crosser. Suddenly she stood up tall and she didn't look old and fragile and frumpy anymore. I could see for a moment what she must have looked like in her prime—small but straight-shouldered, slim, and strong. Her voice was clear, without its usual phlegmy undertones, as she spoke into the microphone, "STOP THIS IMMEDIATELY! I order it. You will cease right now, every last one of you, and listen to me!" And, oddly enough, everyone did. "I've lived in this town all my life. I was born here ninety-four years ago. This town is my community. No one here seems to have the least idea what that means."

The room was silent now. People stood there dripping chocolate sauce and listening.

"I'll tell you what a community is. It's the people who live with you. Period. Some of you think you can pick and choose who is going to be in your community.

You'd miss out on a lot if you could. That's not a community. It takes time to know about folks. You don't
know what all you are yourself; you find out as you go
along. I've been around long enough to know. If someone moves in, why, they're a part of your community
and it's that darn simple. When I grew up here there
wasn't even a town, just a few homesteads and a lot of
fields. You were derned lucky if you had a neighbor to
talk to. You didn't go running around like a chicken
with its head cut off, trying to decide if they were this
or that or the other enough for you. You were just glad
to have a neighbor, that's all. Maybe there's a few
things about these circus people you don't know that
you oughta. Take the Halibuts—Mrs. Halibut used to
be the Governor of Oregon. How many of you knew
that? And Mr. Halibut got the Purple Heart in the last
war, whichever one that was, they do so run together
in my mind. The Gambinis now—sure they throw your
kids around from roofs, which, judging from what I see
of some of the kids around here, can only improve
them—why, each one of those Gambinis has pledged
to donate an organ should the need arise. They're most
of them missing a kidney or something vital even as we
speak! Mrs. Gambini's gotten rid of most of hers, the
only thing left is that insulin thing . . . what's that insulin thing?"

"Pancreas!" shouted someone from the audience.
Oh, she had them in the palm of her hand now.

"I bet you didn't know that Mrs. Wydel invents per-
fume. She has more bottles of scent in her drawers

than anyone you ever saw. And Mr. Wydel captains submarines in his spare time. Both of them have been accepted into the space program. And the snake lady, well, I saved the best for last. The snake lady . . ."

By now, we were hanging on her every word. Unfortunately, we were doomed to hang there forever, because at that moment Mrs. May, looking glorious in a wild-eyed kind of way, had a heart attack and died.

Eighteen

AS YOU CAN IMAGINE, after that, it was pandemonium. Paramedics were called, and after a while they took away poor Mrs. May. Everyone felt guilty. I guess we all had something to feel guilty for, and Reverend Dwindle sat slumped on a chair by the microphone as people kept edging up to confess to him that they thought it was their fault Mrs. May had died. Finally, Reverend Dwindle, who had had enough for one day, said, "For God's sake, it's no one's fault. The woman was ninety-four years old!" Unfortunately, he was a bit too close to the microphone, so everyone heard. There probably would have been a lot of whispered comments about his cold heart and stuff, but I think we were all sick of malicious whispering by then. Instead, a kind of silence hung over the church hall as we cleaned up the mess and wiped pudding off the wall.

No one ever knew why Mrs. May made up all those lies about the circus people, because of course none of it was true. Maybe she was trying to help smooth their way into the community, or maybe she had started lying and discovered she liked it. It didn't matter anyway, because what she did changed our church and the town forever. We knew that the gist of what she said was right, even if the facts were a bit off. We *did* all have to live together, so we might as well learn how to do it and enjoy it, too. But, for some of us, it would have to be one person at a time. I went to find Alfred.

"Come on, Alfred, let's go home," Mr. Halibut was saying just as I got to them. And I knew by the way he said it that they weren't going to leave town after all.

Nineteen

"*WELL,*" *I SAID* to Alfred when he came over the next day and we had done a thorough rehash of the previous day. "Now that the excitement's over, we can finally get back to our books."

"I've finished mine already," he said and took a thick manuscript out of his knapsack and dropped it at my feet.

I was a little annoyed. How dare he be so prolific during my dry spell?

"It's a clever account of the events since I moved here, fictionalized of course. Told in *your* voice."

"Listen, Alfred," I said uneasily, "I don't know if I like that."

"Serves you right," said Alfred. "Now look who's

fictional. Don't worry. For the most part, you come off pretty well."

"Harumph!" I said. "Well, you may still be fictional, for all we know. I never did decide that for sure one way or the other."

"Oh, nonsense," said Alfred. "If I was fictional, then sooner or later, like every book, there would have to be an end."

I looked up at the spring clouds floating in the soon-to-be-summer sky and said, "I guess you have a point at that."